FLYNN

Kate Allenton

Discover other titles by Kate Allenton

At

www.kateallenton.com

ISBN-13: 978-1-944237-09-7
ISBN-10: 1-944237-09-7

ACKNOWLEDGMENTS

I'd like to acknowledge my
READERS....You all rock.
Thank you for taking a chance on my
books.

1 CHAPTER

Mia stepped off the elevator into the dimly lit concrete parking garage, the dark and dingy concrete space not the best choice she'd ever made, but it was convenient. Her quick trip to the mall, for last-minute items for the Island, had seemed like a good idea at the time. She hadn't expected it to take so long; the delay was all in part to one register being down and a lady hogging the other. Goosebumps rose on Mia's arms while scanning the breeding ground for potentially unseen problems. Gas fumes and leaked oil permeated the air. The atmosphere had her clutching her purse close, and she drew in a deep breath, forbidding herself to tremble. The metal from her keys dug into her palm as she poised her finger on top of the pepper spray dispenser, ready to fire. Her gut clenched, and her heart raced. Her assailant was here. First the break-ins at her apartment, and now, here in the shadows. Her skin crawled, unsure if he was waiting and watching in the shadows.

She held the pepper spray against her heart with her finger on the trigger, straining to listen for clues to his hiding spot. This game of cat and mouse left her drained, keeping her off balance and instilled with fear. She had one week left, and she'd be able to breathe again. The muscles in her shoulders tightened as she prepared, ready to fight.

"I can do this," she whispered, lifting her chin with confidence while ignoring her trembling hands.

The elevator doors slid closed, and with it, the ability to flee to the warmth and security the building offered.

Fog rolled in through the concrete opening, blocking the picturesque water from her view. The sunny afternoon sky was replaced with clouds and darkness. The dampness chilled her skin and seeped into her bones.

"I know you're here," she hollered and listened as her voice echoed through the building. "You might as well come out."

She strained, listening to the silence that surrounded her. The sound of an oncoming car engine had her stepping back when it appeared from around the corner and continued down the concrete ramp.

"Get a grip," she whispered to herself and placed one foot in front of the other heading toward her parked car. Fear coupled with anger propelled her determination. "I'm losing my mind." The thought that it was all in her head left her feeling more confident with each step. She clicked the unlock button and reached for the door.

Mia spotted a movement out of the corner of her eye, turning moments before pain exploded in her head, radiating throughout her body. She fell to her knees as her vision blurred and she felt the purse being yanked from her arm. Her eyes rolled in her head as she slowly succumbed to the consuming darkness.

****

Mia woke to the sounds of Trent's voice. Her tight throat and thick tongue stifled her attempt to speak. His comforting hand squeezed hers, and she fought to open her eyes. Pain seared her head from the bright overhead light, making her turn away. Her stomach rolled with the jerky movement.

Within seconds, his hand slipped free from hers and she heard the faint click of the light switch in the room. The light seeping into her lids vanished.

"I turned it off," Trent whispered, taking her hand again.

She opened her eyes again and turned her head toward the beeping sound of the monitors attached to her body. *The hospital?* The smell of antiseptic and cleaning supplies stung her nose. She sighed in resignation. Her quick trip had cost her.

"What happened?"

"You got mugged and knocked unconscious."

She squeezed her eyes closed. "What did they take?"

"Your purse."

She opened her eyes and turned toward her brother before reaching for her neck, which was bare. "Did they take my pendant?"

He gestured with his head toward the table. "It's in the bag with your belongings."

Thank God for small miracles. The pendant contained the backup drive for her research. She never left home without it. Her brows dipped as she held his gaze. "If I didn't have any ID, how did the hospital know to call you?"

"Your ex-boyfriend, the detective, was in the ER when the ambulance arrived. He called me."

She gave a slow nod. Detective Stan Richards knew everything about her case with the break-ins and threats. He was the one she'd called when her life had turned into a creepy case of *CSI*. She had dated the man for six months, and he was the only cop that knew what she was going through. Their parting had been as inevitable as her move.

"I guess he'll be happy I'm leaving town," she teased, trying to lighten the mood.

"I didn't tell him." Trent pressed his lips together. The air in the room turned thick with his concern. "The fewer people, who know you're moving to the Island, the better. Are you sure I can't talk you into staying with me and letting Bruno be your bodyguard?"

"My research is too important. My breakthrough is just around the corner. I can't quit now."

"You can't blame me for trying."

"And you can't blame me for wanting to go." She smiled and squeezed his hand. "Just look at it this way. I'm leaving my problems behind and getting a fresh start. No rat bastard exes, no threats, no one gunning for me."

"Since they took your car keys and have your house key, you'll be staying with me until we can get you out of here. Arguing is futile."

"Okay." The words slipped from her lips as the pain in her head intensified into a migraine. "I'm ready to enjoy life again, without being scared."

2 CHAPTER

Flynn leaned back against the bar and lifted the beer bottle to his lips. The amber liquid was refreshing and everything he needed as it slid down his throat. Several groups were on the dance floor of the Double D, swaying to the enticing rhythm. The vibration rattled the wooden bar behind him. He wasn't there to get drunk, just to blow off aggravation caused by a long week of planning.

A brunette caught his gaze from across the room. Her black dress clung to her body, leaving little to the imagination. Her hair was in that messy style that made a woman look sultry. She licked her red painted lips, and he watched the sway of her hips with each step she took. With a single wink, she slid up next to him at the bar and lifted her hand, ordering two shots of vodka. She slipped her bills on the bar and picked up both shots, turning to face Flynn.

"Flynn Love." Her voice purred as she held out the shot.

Hearing his name on her lips brought him up short. His brows dipped as he took the glass from her hand. "What are celebrating, baby?"

Her lips twitched, and her eyes sparkled. Stepping between his parted legs, she slid her hand up his chest. "Freedom."

Leaning her soft body into his, she held her lips a mere inch from his as her fingers toyed with his hair, heating his body with pure unadulterated lust.

"What are you free from?" he asked, trying as he might to figure out if he'd seen her before.

"The past," she answered with humor in her eyes. "You don't remember me, do you?"

Flynn hated moments like this. Not that he'd had many, but in his younger years, he might have had a one-night stand or two where the woman left his bed before he even remembered her name. Flynn turned his head and downed his shot, placing the glass and his beer on the bar behind him before resting his hands on her waist. "We haven't met." He grinned. "There's no way in hell I would have forgotten a woman as beautiful as you, even if I'd been three sheets to the wind."

Her smile grew as she placed her glass to her lips and tossed back the shot. She wrinkled her nose as she swallowed. Her tongue eased between her lips and she licked the remaining drop of alcohol. His cock hardened against his zipper. He might not have known this woman before she approached, but he'd soon rectify that.

"You sound so sure of yourself." She leaned around him and placed her glass on the counter before resuming her position and entwining her arms around his neck.

"That's because I am." He pulled her closer to his body. The floral scent of her perfume drifted to his nose, teasing and taunting him.

His body tingled, and not because of their proximity. He could feel the premonition coming on fast, like a ticking time bomb, and he was unequipped to stop it. Without fail, his gift would turn into a curse at the most inappropriate time. He closed his eyes, trying unsuccessfully to block the images about to ruin this moment.

Visions of the woman in his arms flashed behind his lids, only they weren't in a bar. They were in a thick of trees, and he was holding her from behind while gripping a gun in his hand.

The scene cut off as fast as it hit. Opening his eyes, he tried to calm his rapid heartbeat. Her brows dipped, the teasing smile gone from her face. "Are you okay?"

Flynn eased her back, reclaiming his personal space. "Who are you?"

She dropped her arms to her sides. "Just a girl who was told you knew how to have a good time. I guess they lied."

She shrugged and swiveled on her high heels. He shot his hand out and grasped her arm, stopping her before she disappeared.

"You're wrong about one thing," he whispered in her ear and moved to stand behind her. He lifted the hair on her shoulders out of his way and placed a kiss on the nape of her neck. His hands caressed her side. "I definitely know how to show a girl a good time." She tilted her head, giving him easy access to her neck. He kissed his way up the ivory path, holding back his grin when her moan slipped free. "I just don't play games."

She lifted her arm and ran her hands through his hair, holding him to her as he nibbled on her ear.

"That's not what I heard." She turned in his arms and pressed her soft, supple breasts against his chest as she worried her bottom lip between her teeth. "I heard you liked to play games and make bets and you lost one a while back." She flashed him a smile. "Five dollars to be exact."

The mystery woman winked and slid out of his grasp, heading for the door. Five dollars? He racked his brain, trying to remember where and when that might have been, trying anything to find a clue that would lead him to her identity.

Flynn brushed the thoughts aside and strolled out into the parking lot. He glanced both ways, looking for any sign of the woman whose neck tasted of strawberries and champagne. She'd disappeared.

****

The next two days flew by while he finalized the touches of the corporate event he'd been planning to help ease his brother-in-law's new employees into Island life. Thoughts of the mystery woman plagued his mind as the days had passed. The party planning had done little to keep his thoughts occupied. Visions of her and the premonition weighed heavy on his mind.

Luke had opened a new lab on the Island within the last year, bringing scientists and staff from the mainland office with him. Flynn's job was simple. Team building in a way that showed the new residents what their

Island had to offer. He was a glorified tour guide, getting paid to play.

Women and men filled the pool area of the hotel and the beach. They were all enjoying the afternoon sun with drinks in their hands, talking and laughing amongst themselves. He glanced at his watch. He still had twenty minutes before the volleyball game started.

Scanning the crowd, he tried to pick out the employees that might not share his enthusiasm for the games he had planned. His gaze landed on the mystery woman from the bar. Her face lay hidden beneath a wide brimmed hat as she sat in the shade, but her body was undeniable. Those were the curves he'd memorized that night. A sarong attached at her waist covered half of her bikini from view. Her chestnut hair hung in a braid down the side over her shoulder. She stood, slipping off her hat and glasses, giving him a glimpse of the porcelain skin. *There you are.*

"My mystery woman." He placed a lazy smile on his face, trying to draw her in with his charm. "I'm afraid you left without telling me your name."

"Did I?" She grinned and slid past him to walk away.

He jogged to get in front of her, stopping her in her path. "You're just going to run again without giving me a hint?" His brows dipped as he studied more than her body this time.

"I didn't run." Her lips quivered as if suppressing a smile. "I just didn't feel the need to tell you nor did I have a reason to stay."

"At least tell me how you knew mine."

She gestured to his body. "Athletic build. You're a jock. A cocky grin from the bar told me that I was not only right but you're a player too." She let her gaze go down his body again. "You're the whole package, bronzed and beautiful, which makes you better than the average bachelor." She let out a sigh and pointed to his hand. "No wedding band or tan lines from removing it tells me you're not married and most likely have commitment issues. With your bone structure, height and looks, I'd guessed early on that you're one of the Love boys I've heard so much about. The fact you were at the bar told me which one."

"What do you mean you've heard?"

"I'm afraid I was part of your bet." She grinned. "I'm Amelia Stewart, Trent's sister." She smiled and patted him on the chest. "But don't worry. You don't have to babysit me. I'm sure I'll find my way around the Island without your help." She wiggled her fingers and stepped around him, heading back into the hotel.

Luke patted his back. "Looks like you crashed and burned."

"Yeah." Flynn let out an aggravated breath. "I never even made it out of the hanger."

"As I recall, you made a promise to her brother, Trent, saying you'd watch out for her." Luke's grin widened, and Flynn's mouth parted.

"That is not the woman Trent described. He said she was timid, nerdy. I imagined her short, wearing thick glasses. I did not imagine that woman." He pointed toward the hotel entrance where she'd disappeared.

"Actually, she is all those things. She's my top analyst. Scored better than I did in college, and she's learning to excel at turning down men." Luke handed Flynn a beer. "I think Trent might have mentioned that she attracts scumbags." Luke chuckled and patted his back. "Have fun with that."

"Sounds like she's got your number." Flynn's brother, Declan, teased as he approached with his arm around his new wife, Olivia's, shoulders.

"Bite me." He didn't know whether to be amused she'd figured him out, or outraged that she considered him so shallow.

"Aw, Flynn." Olivia rubbed his arm. "Don't take it personally. Not all women can swoon at your feet. There are a few of us left that still have functioning brains in our head."

Flynn tsked. "I remember not too long ago that you came needing my help."

"Momentary lapse in judgment." She grinned, even though her cheeks flushed pink. "But don't worry. We'll invite her to family lunch on Sunday and you can win her over at the dinner table and keep up the Love men tradition." Olivia winked.

"Oh no." Flynn threw up his hands. "That's my personal sanctuary. No woman I date will ever breach those walls."

"We'll just have to see about that." Declan took a swig of his beer. "I think it's time to return the favor for the hell you put me through with Olivia. As I seem to recall...you turned Trent onto Olivia just to make me see the light of day."

"Well, it worked, didn't it?"

Declan kissed Olivia's head. "Even still... a promise is a promise. Time to pay the piper."

****

Mia stepped out onto the hotel balcony overlooking the pool and rested her elbows on the railing, watching her coworkers having fun. The hotel offered a temporary solution to her home problem while she was house-hunting. Her boss, Luke Tanner, and his new wife, Skylar, had insisted she stay at the family-owned hotel until she found a more permanent place to lay her head. Flynn was standing right where she'd left him. Only now Luke, Skylar, and another couple clustered around him at the pool. That night at the club, she'd made a spontaneous decision after seeing a picture of the man she'd been told to trust. What she hadn't been expecting was that, in person, sex appeal oozed from him in waves. His testosterone levels were off the chart. It was a shame she couldn't run tests. She built her theory and tested him, teasing and flirting, feeling much more relaxed being away from her nightmare on the mainland. For the first time since she could remember, she'd gone out with her co-workers to experience the Island nightlife. She had a gut feeling, if he was anything like what her brother had described, she'd run into him quickly in that atmosphere and she'd been right. She'd spotted Flynn at the bar.

"Typical guy. Five more minutes and I'd bet money that he'd be trying to get up my skirt." She shook her head as her phone vibrated on the table nearby.

She glanced at the caller ID and answered, pressing the phone to her ear. "It's been less than a week."

"I know," her brother, Trent, said. "But you should have expected my call."

"I did." Mia smiled as she sat in one of the balcony chairs. "I'm surprised you didn't come with me."

"If I could have found a way out of training camp, you know I would have been there until you got settled."

"I guess that's the price you pay for being a hotshot quarterback."

"Have you met Flynn?"

"Yep, sure did," she answered as her gaze fell on the sexy man leading some of her co-workers down to the beach while tossing a volleyball up in the air and catching it. "Skylar has already invited me to her parents' for lunch on Sunday. She wouldn't take no for an answer."

"Good. The Loves are good people, and I trust them."

Trust wasn't something that either Trent or she found easy. Not with the crap they'd been through during their life. She could count on one hand the people she trusted, and it was no wonder, considering all she'd endured in her short life. She turned her back to the ocean and stepped back into her room. "I'll be fine, quit worrying. I haven't had any incidents since I stepped foot on thc Island."

"Let's hope it stays that way."

"I've got to shower and get changed. My meeting with the realtor is in forty minutes.

I'm sure you'd like somewhere to sleep when you come to visit."

Trent chuckled. "Make sure it's got reliable security. If not, you'll need to install it."

"I know," she answered in resignation. "Solid doors, tight security, lighting, safe neighborhood on the Island. You've drilled it into my head."

"A safe room would be nice."

"I'll add it to your wishlist, although I'm not sure anything like that exists on this Island."

"It wouldn't hurt to ask."

"I'm hanging up now. I love you."

"Love you too. Let me know if you have any problems using the money from your trust."

"I'm not using that money," she tsked. "I'm renting. Now get off the phone and go tackle someone."

"Quarterbacks don't tackle, Mia."

"They do if your throw is intercepted and you're the last roadblock between the goal and the other team scoring."

"That's assuming my pass gets picked off."

"It could happen. Bye now. Love you," she rushed to say before disconnecting the call.

Mia walked to the balcony once again and glanced down. The crowd full of Loves had moved on, but that wasn't what caught her attention. A man standing on the other side of the pool, near the plotted ferns, stuck out like a sore thumb. His dark pants and dress shirt made him appear out of place on the hot sunny afternoon. Shades covered his eyes as he stood with his arms crossed and his head tilted up, looking at the balconies and ignoring the flurry of activity by the pool. A shiver skirted down her spine as she stood frozen, staring at the man. Was it possible it was him? She'd been slowly dropping her guard. It couldn't be the guy tormenting her. Could it?

Mia swallowed around the lump in her throat and refused to drop her gaze. If it was him, she wouldn't show weakness. Not here. He gave a simple nod, and her stomach rolled in response. Her phone rang, making her jump. She glanced down at the caller ID to see that Luke was calling, and as she answered, she returned her gaze to where the overly dressed man stood. He was gone.

"Hey, Luke."

"I wanted to remind you about lunch tomorrow."

"I haven't forgotten." She turned, walking back into her room, and pulling the blinds closed; she blocked out the sun.

"Good. I'll pick you up and you can ride with me."

3 CHAPTER

Mia sat impatiently on the stone bench outside the hotel, tapping her foot against the concrete sidewalk, watching guests come and go. Butterflies danced in her belly as she scanned the faces of the men that came and went from the hotel. Each time, she wondered if one these strangers might be him.

"Get a grip," she whispered to herself as another group passed. *I need to find a place away from all these people.* House hunting the day before had been a bust. She was nowhere close to finding a place of her own, yet her search for the day was on hold, thanks to Luke. Attending an afternoon lunch with her boss, and his family, didn't even remotely sound appealing.

The black SUV pulled up right on time. She was surprised to find Luke getting out and to see the passenger seat empty. Luke opened her door. "Skylar is meeting us there. She has a Sunday morning ritual with Olivia to shop for new items for their store."

Mia tried to hide her reluctance behind her smile. "You know, this isn't necessary. I don't want to intrude on the family lunch. I can just grab a bite to eat at the diner."

"Don't be silly." He shut the door, jogged around to the driver's seat and slid behind the wheel. "I grew up at the Loves' house. Sky's brother, Declan, and I have been best friends since grammar school. The family is great. You're going to love them."

She clicked her seatbelt into place. "Do you always bring coworkers to your family functions?"

He glanced her way and grinned. "Nope, but seeing as how the Loves know Trent, they insisted. They have this habit of picking up strays and adopting them." He glanced at her as he pulled out onto the main street. "Don't take that the wrong way. I was a stray too."

Just peachy. Mia turned toward the oceanfront, watching the waves hit the beach on the scenic route. "I'm eager to get back to work. I'm close to a breakthrough of the molecular structure of XRP. I'm on the verge of a potential antidote for the cure, ready for human trials when we secure approval."

He parked behind another SUV in front of a large ranch-style home and killed the ignition. "I thought you might be getting close. Let me know when you're done, and I'll start the approval process."

She gave him a genuine smile as she got out of the SUV at the same time Skylar pulled up behind them. She and another woman got out. Luke introduced the other woman as Olivia, Skylar's business partner and Declan's wife. Both women were stunning, and from what Mia had already heard about Skylar, she was down to earth. Her kind of people.

Music played from the backyard as white smoke billowed above the house. Skylar's eyes lit up as she wound her arm around Mia's, and Olivia took the other side.

"You're in for a treat. They made barbecue."

****

Flynn's parents danced around the backyard to the music coming from the speakers during their Sunday ritual. He threw the football in a perfect spiral to Declan, who caught the ball, tossed it to the ground, and crossed the yard toward his wife. Flynn's lips thinned with irritation, and he cursed whichever brother arranged for Trent's sister to be invited. *There goes my sanctuary.* Flynn plastered a fake smile on his lips as he crossed the yard.

"Welcome to our home," his mom called out with open arms, pulling Mia into her embrace. "We're so glad you could come."

"Thank you for having me." Mia's cheeks tinted in embarrassment. Her whole demeanor was quite the opposite of the vixen he'd met in the club and the sharp-tongued woman at the pool.

"Marvin, dear, this is Trent's baby sister. I'm sure you've seen her at the hotel."

"Of course. It's lovely to finally be able to put a face with the name. Skylar and Luke have told us so much about you."

"Have they?" Mia glanced at Luke.

"Oh yes, Luke told us you're brilliant. Smarter than even he is, and that you're close to a breakthrough on an extremely stubborn project."

"You did?"

"Guilty as charged," Luke answered before addressing the rest of the family. "She is single-handedly creating a vaccine that will save lives."

"Hopefully." She blushed. "And I can't take all the credit. I have an extremely bright team that helps."

Well, well, well, this woman was a conundrum of sorts. Attracts sleazebags, smart as a whip, a genius in the lab, and she was modest. From what he could tell, the woman needed no help, except maybe a wing woman in the clubs to reel her in from teasing strangers. She caught his stare, and he smiled and gave her a slight nod.

It was at that moment, in the gleam of her eyes that he finally understood. Mia Stewart was street smart, and he'd been outplayed. She could be anyone to anybody, if the setting and the mood fit her.

Flynn's dad and Declan pulled the barbecue off the smoker and disappeared inside with everyone following behind. Flynn touched her arm, meeting her gaze. "Can I speak to you for a moment?"

"Sure." Her smile hinted toward a smirk.

"Luke, we'll be inside in a minute."

Luke glanced at Mia, who gave a quick nod before Luke acknowledged and disappeared into the house.

Flynn steered her farther away from the French doors to the side of the house. He inhaled a deep breath before he spoke.

"Is this a game to you?" He narrowed his eyes. "First you come on to me at the bar, knowing full well who I am, then you ignore me at the pool, and now you show up at my parents' house." He took a deep calming

25

breath. "I only promised to show you around the Island and keep you out of trouble."

"Someone finally told you who I was." Mia's cheeks reddened, but she cupped his cheek and patted it, never backing down from his glare. She lifted her chin and poked his chest. Hard. "I didn't ask for a babysitter. I don't need a babysitter, and if I did, my brother sure as hell wouldn't have picked a playboy like you to do the job."

Flynn's eyes narrowed. "So what? I'm no angel. I never claimed to be, but you're forgetting one important thing."

"Yeah, what's that?"

"You're the one who came on to me." With every word he spoke, he stepped forward, and she stepped back until her back was pressed against the house.

"It was a test, Flynn, in which case, you failed miserably. Unlike you, I don't need another notch on my bedpost, and if I'd actually been attracted to you, I would have left with you that night. Don't think I didn't see you come after me." She shook her head. "I know your type. Hell, I've dated enough of your type to be an expert. You're no different. I didn't ask for this; I didn't ask for you, and I damn sure didn't ask to be here."

Flynn rested his hand above her head, trapping her against the building as he stepped closer to her, closing the gap between their bodies. "You're quick to judge, darling." His lips twisted in a smile as he leaned into her space. "What about getting all the facts for an intelligent hypothesis? That must only extend to your work."

Mia inhaled a deep breath, glancing up at him from beneath hooded eyes.

"You were part of a deal, nothing more, nothing less," he whispered against her lips. "Having met you... It appears I got the short end of the stick."

The slap came quick and fast against his cheek before she shoved him away. Fire lit her eyes.

Flynn held up his hands and stepped back. He deserved it, or worse. This wasn't the way he treated women. He expected to see hatred in her eyes, but what he found surprised him even more. Fear. "Why don't we just start over?"

She shook her head. "Don't bother. You just confirmed my theory."

"So you did have a theory...about me?"

"Yeah, one that concludes you to be a self-centered, egotistical, jack—"

Her words were cut off as Skylar rounded the corner.

"Jackass. Yep, that's my brother. He can't seem to help himself." Skylar shot him a glare and linked arms with Mia, pulling her away.

"I'm so sorry. You'll have to forgive him. I think he was adopted."

Flynn followed behind them into the house where the others were already seated at the dinner table. His mother raised a disapproving brow. He knew that look, and he knew the ass-chewing coming later.

His mother rose, prepared a plate of ribs with all the fixings, and then set it down in front of Mia before retaking her seat. "So, Mia, Luke tells us you haven't been having any luck while apartment hunting."

"No, ma'am. With all of the new lab employees that moved to the Island, I'm afraid there's not much available since I got a late start." Mia reached for her glass of sweet tea.

His mother gave a small shake of her head before she took a bite of her potato salad.

"Flynn has space," his father announced.

Mia's eyes widened. The horror on her face was priceless. "Oh no, I couldn't..."

Flynn's lips twitched. He was amused by her reaction. He placed his elbows on the table and clasped his fingers together, knowing his insistence would agitate her more. He could kill two birds with one stone. Watch her like a hawk, and figure out what the hell he'd seen in her eyes. "You know, Dad, that's a perfect idea."

Mia whipped her gaze to him. "You must be joking." She turned back to Flynn's mother.

"I'm sure I'll find something. I'd hate to put Flynn out when I'd be leaving at the first vacancy available."

Declan leaned back in his seat, his arm around Olivia's chair. "I think that's a wonderful idea." Declan gave Flynn a shit-eating grin. "Considering he told Trent he'd show her around the Island and she doesn't know anyone. I think it's the hospitable thing to do."

"I'm nothing if not hospitable." Flynn held his arms open and winked at her.

She rolled her eyes, and he held in his chuckle.

Skylar reached for Mia's hand and patted it. "Don't worry, it's not as bad as it seems. What my dad means is that Flynn has an efficiency apartment over his garage. It isn't much, and it only has a small kitchen, but it can be your own space until you find something else. I'm sure you'll barely cross paths."

Flynn picked up a rib and held it in front of his mouth. "I'm sure you're right, Sky. We probably won't run into each other much after I do my duty of showing her around, as I promised. You know I'd never welch on my word."

"How about I give you your five bucks back and we call it even?" Mia narrowed her eyes.

"You don't have my five bucks. Your brother does."

Mia frowned, and her face pinched. The little vixen was searching for a rebuttal in her overactive mind. He'd teased her enough. Granted, she'd played him, but he would be the better person today... well, starting now, anyway. He held her gaze. "Mom, I'm afraid I understand her hesitancy. When we first met, I was kind of an ass."

His mother's eyes narrowed.

"Kind of?" Sky batted her eyes all innocently.

"Language, Flynn. There are women around the table," his father scolded.

"These women swear worse than I do." He grinned.

"We do not." Skylar launched a roll across the table, hitting him in the head.

"But you did teach me better manners than Sky is showing." He glanced at Mia. "I am truly sorry for letting your beauty cloud my actions." He held his hand to his chest in mock sincerity. "I only hope we can move past our initial meeting and try to be friends."

A slew of emotions crossed her face while she watched the family members, at the table, ignoring their lunches as their eyes glanced between her and Flynn.

Mia cleared her throat. "You do realize that I'll be coming and going at all hours of the night and day. My schedule varies, depending on the advancements and progressions I make."

Flynn held in a grin as she tried for an easy way out. "I'm not your warden or your parent, Mia. Heck, I'm hardly there myself."

Mia glanced around the table once more to find everyone looking at her. She was stuck, and he knew it. Mia Stewart and all of her secrets were about to be his roommate.

"Fine."

"Great, now that's settled, let's eat." Declan reached across the table, snagged a roll and set it on Olivia's plate next to the other two. He was wrapped so tightly around Olivia's fingers that Flynn swore he'd never end up the same way.

4 CHAPTER

Flynn offered to drive Mia back to the hotel so she could pack her things and they could get her situated before that evening. She'd been hesitant getting in the car, but she lifted her chin and slid inside. Almost as if she was proving something to herself. The air between them was charged in a way he couldn't pinpoint. A way that no other woman had ever made him feel.

He followed her up to her room and lounged on the patio, out of her way, looking down at the pool while she gathered her things and repacked her suitcase.

Flynn leaned against the railing, watching the surf roll onto the shore. "I don't blame you for wanting to stay here," he called out over his shoulder. "I would hate giving up this view, too, but trust me when I tell you that mine is just as great."

He turned to find her leaning against the sliding glass door, her packed suitcase at her feet, fiddling with the necklace hanging around her neck. "I'll just be glad to get settled somewhere." She stepped out on the balcony. "You're a smart guy. You do realize this is a terrible idea, right?"

"Don't worry, Mia. I'm not going to sneak into your room. You've made it clear that I'm not your type." The smile grew on his face. "Your brother warned me that you only date assholes."

"Did he?" Mia spun around and picked up her suitcase. "Well, that would put you on the top of the list."

Oh, she was going to be fun to play with. She gave as good as she got, and he'd just begun testing her limits and her resolve. Flynn moved to the door, holding it open, and took the suitcase from her hands. Winning her over would be a piece of cake, if she didn't kill him in his sleep. This woman would be putty in his proverbial hands, and what better way to watch out for her than to watch her every move?

****

Mia's hair whipped around her face and into her mouth on the ride in Flynn's Jeep. She didn't have enough hands or a hat to keep it from attacking her head. Flynn drove without a care in the world. By the time she got to his place, her hair would be one big hornet's nest of tangles and she'd be in deep need of a shower to get rid of the dirt residue and salty air clinging to every pore in her skin.

"How far out do you live?" she hollered into the wind, unsure if he'd heard her.

"We'll be there in a few minutes."

A few minutes turned out to be more like twenty. With each bend in the dirt road they were on, she worried if her little car could even make the trip up and down these roads or if she'd get stuck.

Flynn pulled into a long driveway that led to a two-story house and killed the ignition. "Home sweet home."

He jumped out of the Jeep and grabbed her bag as she slid out of the passenger side. Her mouth parted as she stood and stared.

"What's wrong?" he asked as he approached her from behind.

"It's beautiful." She smiled and drew in a deep breath of fresh air. The landscape wasn't anything she'd ever seen. The house was a hidden oasis, complete with a crystal blue lake in the backyard. There were in their own private jungle with wildflowers and nature surrounding them.

"I bet you were expecting something small and in town next to the action." He jogged up the steps to the front door.

"I don't know what I was expecting, but it wasn't this." She paused on the porch. "Didn't they say you have an efficiency apartment above the garage?"

Flynn grinned. "What they didn't tell you is that I'm using it for storage since the plumbing doesn't work." He slid the key into the lock and pushed the door open, letting her walk in first. "The house is plenty big for the both of us. We're even sleeping on different floors. My room is on the first floor, and the guest rooms are upstairs, so you'll have all the privacy you need."

"Flynn...I couldn't possibly..."

"We'll call it my penance for being a jackass."

Flynn ignored her further protests and jogged up the stairs, leaving her words to fall on deaf ears. She was helpless to do anything but follow. She found him waiting outside one of the rooms on the backside of the house with the door open.

"I'm putting you in the upstairs master. I think you'll be comfortable in here."

She stepped into a room that was bigger than her apartment back on the mainland. It wasn't the size that had her mouth dropping open; it was the floor-to-ceiling windows and doors that ran along the back wall. The blinds were open and she had a full view of the sun as it was dipping behind the horizon.

"Why isn't this your bedroom?" She opened the sliding glass doors and stepped out onto the balcony. "If I lived here, I'd never leave."

Flynn set her bag down and walked out on the balcony with her. He leaned over the railing and pointed below. "My room is beneath this one. I get antsy at night, and it's just easier for me to step outside being down there. When I can't sleep, I go for a swim. It helps me to relax." He turned and leaned against the railing to look at her. "It's just easier that way."

She bit her lip when reality and common sense hit her. "I'm going to have to find another place. My car won't be here for a week, and even then, I don't think it will make it down that road. I think I'm better off at the hotel." She held his gaze. "Maybe you should take me back."

"Your car will be fine, trust me," he said as he walked back into the room. "Let me give you the rest of the tour, and then you can get settled in. Come on..."

She followed him as he pointed out some of the things in her room. The master suite had a master bath with floor-to-ceiling tile. There was a separate shower that had several overhead sprays and a Jacuzzi bath tub that could host a party of four. Hell, he'd probably had orgies in that room.

Downstairs, he pointed out the kitchen and did a quick tour of where he kept the dishes.

"Don't take this the wrong way, but isn't my presence going to throw a wrench in the whole bachelor angle you're working? "

He chuckled without reply.

"My room is a replica of yours. But this is my favorite spot," he said as he opened a door off the living room and stepped outside into a screened-in area. A hot tub sat in a darkened corner with candles around the rim.

"I'm sure it is." She walked over and ran her hands through the warm water. "I bet you entertain a lot."

"Are you basing that off of assumptions or your findings?"

"It's a luxurious home." She turned to find him watching her. "You have all the luxuries of a bachelor, and why wouldn't you show it off? I'm sure you worked hard for this lifestyle."

He gave a slow nod. "For a scientist, I would have pegged you for more of a person looking to discover the truth instead of using your imagination." He frowned. "Why don't you go get settled, and I'll see if I can find my spare key."

"Do cabs come out this far? I still have a week before my car is brought over."

"You worry too much."

"And you don't worry enough," she called out to his retreating back.

****

Mia woke refreshed as the morning sunlight rose over the pond and caressed her cheek. She slid out of the bed, opened the balcony door, and stepped outside, resting her arms on the railing. She'd thought seeing the lake and surrounding forest was amazing at night. She was mesmerized by the sun-drenched colors around her. A smile formed on her lips as she scanned the area and noticed Flynn already out for a morning swim. He was like a piece of the ambiance, fitting in as if nature itself had invited him to play. He belonged here...and in another world, another setting, this would be her ideal place. She sighed and watched as he stepped out of the lake, grabbing his towel from the shore. He ran the cotton over his head and face and wiped it down his abs. He lifted his gaze to meet hers and a smile splayed across his lips.

"Good morning," he called out.

"Do you always swim in the morning?"

"Morning, noon, or night. There's nothing better. Take your shower and come down. I'll fix you some coffee and breakfast and then tell you what I have planned for the day. Before you protest, which I know you were about to do, I won't take no for an answer."

She hesitated briefly before giving in and watched him disappear back into his room. Stranded on an Island, with no transportation in the middle of paradise with Flynn, wasn't a hardship. He was beautiful in the way that made a scientist want to study his body and face proportions. Mia took her time getting dressed and then headed downstairs. He'd said he had plans for them, yet her only goal was finding a place of her own, so she could finally get settled. She had only one week left before she had to show up at work, and she would need all that time to find a place and get her stuff shipped over. Time was ticking like a bomb.

She bounced off the last stair while sliding her phone into her back pocket before turning the corner into the kitchen, following the aroma of freshly brewed coffee. Flynn stood in front of the stove, shoeless and shirtless, wearing nothing more than a pair of gym shorts as he cooked. Heat pooled in her belly as she watched the play of his muscles while he worked. She bit her lip and leaned against the doorway, taking a minute to allow herself this guilty pleasure of admiring him without his big mouth getting in the way.

"You like what you see?" he asked without turning around.

The moment fled when the first syllable left his delicious lips.

"I've seen better," she lied and pushed off the doorframe, stepping into the kitchen. She started rooting around in the cabinets, looking for coffee cups.

He reached around her, opened up another door, pulled one out, and handed it to her, never missing a stride in what he'd been doing.

She made her coffee and leaned her hip against the counter, watching as he finished making scrambled eggs and bacon. "You know, this really is unnecessary. If you can just take me back to town, I can rent a car and get back to the hunt for my own place."

"Why would you do that?" he asked, glancing over his shoulder at her for the first time. "Free room and board plus you get the added pleasure of seeing me every day."

She grabbed a piece of bacon and walked over to the table. "Anyone ever tell you that you're full of yourself?"

"All the time." He grinned and slid the food onto two waiting plates and handed her one. "Mainly my family though. The women I date don't seem to mind."

"That says a lot about them and you."

He smiled, sat down opposite her, and took a bite of his eggs. She watched, mesmerized, as he slid the tines of the fork out of his mouth. No man had ever had this effect on her. She was losing her mind, or more likely, more of her brain cells were evaporating the longer she stayed in his presence. Her IQ was dropping with every second that passed. It was official. She couldn't stay.

"What's the matter? You don't like eggs?"

She shook the haze from her mind as her cheeks heated. "Eggs are fine." She picked up her fork and stabbed some. "You must secrete an extra dose of pheromones. That's the only explanation I can think of."

"Excuse me?" he asked as his lips tilted at the corners.

"The way you" — she waved her fork in the air toward him — "draw women in and hold their attention. That's the only answer I can come up with. You should get that tested," she mentioned nonchalantly, as if she'd been discussing his blood pressure.

"You say that like it's a bad thing."

She swallowed her bite of eggs. "It is."

"I haven't had any complaints." He bit into his bacon. "So...you find me irresistible, do ya? I can work with that. Maybe you aren't as immune to my charms as you claim to be."

"Oh, I am. Your charm takes a nose dive when you open your mouth and turn pompous."

"Ouch." He held his hand to his chest as if she'd stabbed him in the heart.

"Oh, don't take it the wrong way. Some women are attracted to self-centered men who ooze sex appeal. It's fascinating really. I'm sure I could pull up a hundred studies done on the phenomena."

"But you're not one?"

She shook her head and took another bite.

"And what if I told you I had brains to match the brawn?"

She tossed her head back and laughed, only stopping when she met his unamused gaze. "You're serious?"

"Why do you have such a low opinion of me?"

Mia rested her fork on her plate, picked up her coffee, and took a sip while she pondered his question. "I guess because not only did you lose a bet with my brother, but you were also such an easy target at the bar. Men have a one-track mind when it comes to sex, and you might as well have had a sign on your forehead that flashed 'one-night stand wanted' in bright neon lights. I guess I expected my brother to pick someone more suited to my needs while I'm here."

Flynn sat back in his chair and held her gaze. She could see the wheels turning in his head, yet he remained quiet for several seconds, which seemed like an eternity. For

43

once since meeting him, she was hoping he'd get agitated and spit out another insult so they'd be even.

"And just what's wrong with enjoying sex?"

"Nothing." She shrugged. "If that's what you're looking for in a relationship, you'll be just fine."

He placed his elbows on the table, laced his fingers together, and met her gaze as if he was seeing clear down to her soul, and knowing him, he probably was. "Why are you here on the Island?"

"What?"

"You seem to think you know all my secrets. I think it's only fair that I know yours, and seeing as I'm too uneducated to figure them out, you might as well go ahead and tell me." He tilted his head. "What are you running from?"

Her mouth parted before she snapped it closed. "I'm not running from anything."

Flynn's jaw ticked, and he narrowed his eyes. "You know, I may not be a human lie detector like my brother, but I'm smart enough to be able to tell that you, my dear Mia, are lying through your pretty little lips." He sat back and sipped his coffee.

"Your brother is a human lie detector?" she asked, choosing to ignore the additional assumptions he'd made.

"He has his moments," Flynn answered, deflecting again, and he switched gears. "People come to the Island to escape their lives, and don't tell me it's because of your job. We both know that Luke offered his employees the choice of working on the mainland or coming here. So again, I ask…why are you here?"

"I don't know what it is that you think you know, but I can assure you that you're wrong."

"Mmm-hmm." Flynn picked up his fork and took another bite of his eggs. "You're right. What do I know? I'm just some jock with a hot body and a mouth that turns you off." He raised a brow and pointed to her plate with his fork. "You should eat before it gets cold. You're going to need the energy for what I have planned for the day."

Mia took a bite of her bacon. Relief flooded her body when he dropped his line of questioning. He was asking things she wasn't ready to answer. No one but the police and her brother knew why she had moved to the Island. No one knew about her past or about the break-ins and mugging. She was here to start a new life. One that didn't include filing a police report every month.

5 CHAPTER

Flynn covertly watched Mia in the passenger seat, and his lips tilted in an amused smile. With her hair up in a ponytail and a baseball cap perched on her head, she was prepared for the wind, or whatever might play havoc in her life. Her hair was just the tip of the iceberg.

"You should let your hair down and live a little," he said while trying to keep a straight face.

She turned her glare on him, and his amused smile widened.

He had her pegged. She liked order and being in control, and in his Jeep, she didn't have that and it aggravated the piss out of her.

Pushing her buttons was easy enough. Keeping her off kilter seemed to be a piece of cake, not that he wasn't intentionally playing games with her, but the girl needed some excitement in her life. He wasn't blind to their chemistry, and she'd soon find out he wasn't stupid either.

He remained quiet and slowed the Jeep when he saw her pull out her cell phone and press it to her ear while using her palm to cover her other ear.

"Trent," she yelled. "I'll have to call you back. I can't hear you."

Her nose squinted as if she was straining to listen before she shrugged and disconnected the call.

"We'll be there in a minute and you can call back," Flynn hollered as he took the last curve, and within minutes, they were pulling into a parking place on Main Street.

"This isn't the car rental," she said as she unbuckled her belt and stepped out of the Jeep.

"I told you, you don't need one. I'll drive you around until your car shows up."

With her lips pressed together, she was hesitant stepping out of the Jeep. He waited for her on the sidewalk and was quick to toss his arm over her shoulder.

"What are you doing?" she asked, trying to roll from beneath his hold.

"Giving you a tour."

She removed his palm from her shoulder. "I'm not your date. I'm your platonic roommate, and even that is temporary."

Platonic, ha, not for long. He kept the comment to himself. "I made a promise to your brother to keep the sleaze bags away." He rested his palm on her shoulder again. "And this is how I work."

"Yeah? I don't think he realized who he was asking."

"Oh, he knew." Flynn grinned while steering her across the street, leading her to Tidal Waves, the boutique Olivia and his sister owned. "This is Skylar and Olivia's place. If you need something girly, this is the place to come."

The bell above the door chimed.

"I don't need anything." She gave him a sideways glance.

"I do," he whispered in her ear. "If you haven't noticed, my sister-in-law is pregnant; Sky and my mom are giving her a shower soon."

"Do you expect Olivia to pick out her own present?"

"Of course not." He led her down the aisle toward the office area. "That's what Sky is for."

"So who's picking out Skylar's present then? Olivia?"

Flynn veered off course and ushered her into an aisle between some tall cases. "What are you talking about? Sky isn't pregnant."

Mia gave him a knowing smile, as if she held the answers to the universe. "I'm a trained observer, Flynn. She has *the glow*. Not only that, did you not notice how Luke was touching her stomach? How he kept putting food on her plate? Not to mention the fact, that, while everyone else was drinking wine or beer, Sky and Olivia drank water or juice." Mia patted his shoulder. "Open your eyes, Flynn, and start paying attention. I'll bet you five bucks that Olivia isn't the only one expecting in your family; your sister is too."

"No way. She'd tell me."

Mia held out her hand. "Five dollars. Is it a bet?"

He was quick to shake her hand.

"There's a sucker born every day. No wonder my brother bets with you." Mia stepped out of the aisle, heading for the door that led to the back office, and Flynn hurried to her side.

"You can't come out and ask her. What if she isn't? She's going to be offended."

"I'm not going to ask her. We'll wait for the announcement." Mia grinned. "She won't be able to contain her excitement much longer."

Mia waited for Flynn to open the employee door and followed him into an office. Olivia was at her desk, and Skylar was leaning against it. Their discussion was halted when Olivia nodded toward them, and Sky glanced over her shoulder.

"I wasn't expecting you until later." Sky managed a smile and pulled her brother in for a hug. "He's not still being an ass, is he?" she asked Mia.

"He has his moments." Mia smiled. "We weren't interrupting, were we?"

"Of course not." Skylar met Olivia's gaze. "We were just talking about how Reed needs to get out from behind his computer and out of the house more."

"I can help with that." Flynn grinned. "I know just how to make that happen." And he did. Nothing that a little R&R Flynn-style couldn't fix.

Skylar pulled a bag out of her desk and handed it to Flynn. "Can you also get Landon to bring his ass back home?"

Flynn's smile fell. His baby brother, Landon, was going through issues. With his heightened senses, his choice of a military career should have been the last job he picked.

"Landon is your other brother?" Mia asked as she glanced between them all.

"Yep, he's currently on assignment God-knows-where, but he hasn't been home in a couple years."

Mia chewed her bottom lip. Flynn knew that sign. The wheels in her over-crowded head were turning again, and there was no telling what was about to pop out of her mouth.

"Did he return for your wedding?" she asked.

"No, the best I got was a congratulatory phone call."

Mia narrowed her eyes and tilted her head. "What was his attitude?"

"Preoccupied, as if he was having a hard time focusing on our conversation and was trying his best to keep something from me. I could hear it in his voice."

She gave a slow nod. "He's withdrawn." She glanced between the siblings. "Look at your data. Has he acted like this before, and if so, what were the circumstances? You guys would know him better than anyone. You figure out what was going on back in previous years, and it should lend credence to what is happening now with him or at least something comparable."

Mia gave a sad smile, as if she'd already figured it out in her mind.

"You're right." Olivia rose and placed her hand on her belly. "He's done this before." She stepped forward. "Don't you remember during his freshman year of college? He acted the same way when he dropped out and joined the military. He avoided everyone's calls for months because he didn't want to come clean."

"So he's hiding something?" Skylar asked, glancing around the room.

"It would explain his absence and reluctance to coming home," Mia suggested.

"But what? What wouldn't he tell us?"

"If you figure that out, you'll get him home."

"What if he was injured? He'd keep that from us." Skylar covered her mouth with her hand. "We need to get him home."

If Landon were injured, it would take an army to bring him back home. His thick head and pride would stand in the way, and with his heightened senses... Flynn and his brothers needed to come up with a plan.

"Find the right triggers to get him home, and don't give him an excuse to back out."

"You sound like a shrink," Olivia added.

She smiled and glanced at Flynn. "I have a dual doctorate in chemistry and psychology."

"Fascinating. Two completely separate fields," Skylar chimed in.

"I like to be well-rounded," Mia answered.

"Of course you do." Flynn wrapped his arm around her shoulder and steered her toward the door. "Come on, Doc. Let's let these two ladies get back to plotting and planning. We've got some tourist things to take care of."

"Great." The word was long and drawn-out with about as much enthusiasm as when she'd agreed to move in with him.

Flynn tossed his arm over her shoulder when they hit the street. His mind was on his brothers as they walked toward the park where he liked to jog, when he didn't swim. Mia didn't push his arm from her shoulder this time. She clutched the locket around her neck as if she, too, was lost in thought. He felt her body stiffen beneath his palm, and her breath hitched, which drew him out of his own thoughts.

He followed her gaze across the street to where a man was standing inside the coffee shop, drinking. Instantly, he was overcome with a vision. She was standing inside talking to him. A tear dripped down her cheek as he watched from outside. His eyes flew open, and he pulled her into the alleyway. "Who is he?"

"Who is who?" she asked innocently.

"The man in the coffee shop." He searched her gaze for answers he wasn't sure he'd get. It was times like this that he wished he had his brother's abilities. Ones that could do more than give him a faint glimpse of what was about to happen.

"I, uh..." She peered out of the alleyway back toward the coffee shop. "I need to talk to him. He's an old friend." She hurried out of the alley and back onto the sidewalk. He quickly followed her across the street, and just like his vision, he waited patiently outside where he could see them talking.

6 CHAPTER

Mia's body seized up the moment she spotted Detective Stan Richards in the coffee shop. He was watching her from inside. The fact that he was on the Island told her as much as she needed to know. He wasn't here in a social capacity. He wasn't here trying to win her back. He was here on official business. She could read it in his face without even asking. She'd seen that look countless times when they had dated. He was all about the job, and it appeared today, the job was her. Her stomach rolled as desperation seeped into her bones; she hoped if she just blinked he'd be gone, nothing more than a figment of her imagination. She hurried across the street and yanked the door open. His normally stoic face softened as she approached.

"How did you find me?" she asked as she neared.

"That doesn't matter." He glanced around, and she felt the first tear escape her eyes. This wasn't happening. Not again. Not here. "Is there someplace private we can talk?"

"I..." She glanced out the window at Flynn waiting. His arms crossed over his chest, and his brow lifted when she met his gaze. "Sure." She turned back to Stan. "How about the park down the street. It's secluded enough to give us some privacy."

He grabbed a file off the table and gestured to the door.

Flynn met them outside. "Everything okay?"

"Yes," she answered.

"Not even close," Stan corrected as he held out his hand. "I'm Detective Richards, and you are?"

"Flynn Love." They shook hands before walking toward the park.

"Boyfriend?" Stan asked Mia.

"Yes," he answered.

"No," she corrected. "Temporary roommate."

Richard's brows dipped, but he questioned no further. Mia held her hand to her stomach as they approached one of the benches.

"Mia, I hope you don't mind my intruding on you, but this couldn't wait. Your brother told me where to find you, but when I stopped by the hotel, they told me you'd checked out."

"I forgot to tell Trent that I'm staying with Flynn."

He gestured for them all to sit at the picnic table, and he slid his file across to her. "We got a hit on your attacker."

Flynn remained silent. Thank God. She couldn't deal with all of this and his questions. Not yet. "What did you find?"

"We tracked your cell phone from when you were mugged. We expected some little punk to have taken it since it didn't happen at your house where the break-ins had occurred. We didn't have any indication that the two were connected."

"But you do now?" Flynn asked trying to get a handle on the situation.

"You can say that," Richards answered as Mia opened the file. Her fingers shook as she reached inside to pull out the contents. She spread out the pictures, and her breath caught in her throat.

The photo in the file taken by the police was a shrine of some sort. The shrine was covered with pictures of her, pictures she never realized were being taken. Some were close-ups, and others were obviously from across the street. A few of them were of her entering her work building, getting in her car, at the gate to her brother's house and even one of her getting on the ferry and hugging her brother goodbye. She could feel her throat closing. Her body visibly trembled as she clenched her fist.

Flynn's palm landed on her back. The familiarity and comfort of his touch, as if lending her the strength she'd need to deal with the evidence. She pushed the thought away to deal with later.

She closed her eyes and shook her head. "He followed me." She opened her eyes and met Richard's gaze. "He knows I'm here."

"I'm afraid so."

"Who?" Flynn asked.

"We're still trying to figure that out," Richards answered. "All the evidence indicates that he was squatting in this house." Stan pointed to one of the pictures. "We traced the property back to McGregor Pharmaceuticals, but they are claiming that it's been vacant for a while and currently on the market."

"Wait...did you say, McGregor?" Flynn asked.

"Yeah, why?" Richards asked.

"McGregor is my brother-in-law, Luke's, chief competitor, and Luke is her boss. Not to mention the fact that his daughter was killed on the Island last year. Do you think this might be work related?"

Mia shook her head. "No one knows what I'm working on, and we don't discuss it outside the office."

"If it's not work, then it's personal?" Flynn asked, and all Mia could do was shrug. She had no idea who was doing this to her or the motivation behind it.

Stan leaned across the table and laid his hand on top of hers. Flynn's hand paused in its rubbing motion. "We're going to find him, Mia. I promise."

She nodded. He'd said the same thing after the break-in. And she had about as much confidence in the police finding the guy as she did when things first started happening. There was no logic behind why she was being stalked or whatever the hell was going on. She couldn't rationalize it any more today than she could that day. "Thanks for coming, Stan."

"I wish it was under better circumstances, Mia. Do you want me to stay with you? I can take some time off if you need me."

"I'll be fine." She gave him a small smile that didn't reach her eyes as she slid her hand free. She stood and pulled out her cell phone. "Excuse me, please. I have to call Trent."

They both nodded as she walked off. She could feel their eyes on her retreating back as she called Trent and held the phone up to her ear. The call went to voice mail. "Trent. He knows I'm on the Island, but don't worry. I'm staying with Flynn, and his place is out in the middle of nowhere. He won't find me there. Stan showed up with new information. They found my phone, and when they did, they found a freakin' shrine. This guy had pictures of me, including one at your gate. Please call me back."

She disconnected the call and turned to find Stan and Flynn in a hushed conversation. The contention between the two was evident. She could feel it from where she stood.

****

"So you're the wannabe boyfriend?" Stan asked.

"And you're the ex," Flynn answered.

"Is she going to be safe with you?"

"Safer than she was on the mainland with you apparently." Flynn crossed his arms and tilted his head. "Why did you come? You could have told her over the phone."

Stan's jaw ticked, and in that minute, Flynn knew that Mia was the one who'd broken things off between the two.

"I wanted to check on her and make sure she was okay."

Flynn gave a knowing nod. He could read between the lines. "I'll take good care of her. Don't you worry about a thing. You should get back and do your job. The sooner you catch this creep, the better it will be for her peace of mind."

Stan's eyes narrowed. "You just want me out of the way, don't ya, Romeo? Worried Mia still might have feelings for me? We do have a past, which is more than I can say for you."

"You might be her past, but I'm her present. There's no competition." Flynn rose, making Stan stand too. "My brother is the local sheriff. I'll update him on what's going on and make sure he gets these pictures."

"Don't bother yourself. I'm heading there next." Stan took the pictures, and they both turned to find Mia stomping over to them.

"I could feel the testosterone from over there. Are you two done with your pissing match?"

Flynn grinned. Mia was a smart cookie. More than book smart, she had street smarts that were showing. "There's no pissing match. Isn't that right, Detective?"

Stan pulled Mia into his arms and looked down into her worried eyes. "I'll be in touch. You know how to reach me."

She nodded, and he leaned down and kissed her cheek. "You remember everything I taught you?"

She pushed against his chest. "Stan, I'm not that same scared woman. I can take care of myself, but thanks for caring."

"Always."

He kissed her forehead before releasing her. Stan eyed Flynn with a smirk on his lips as he walked off with the file in hand. Flynn's blood boiled. This guy was an arrogant little prick.

"Let's get out of here." Flynn spoke with a deceptive calm as he tossed his arm over her shoulder again. This time, it wasn't in play or in gest to push her buttons. After seeing those pictures, he was genuinely concerned. He leaned down and whispered, "You should have told me."

"I know," she whispered under her breath, just loud enough for him to hear.

Lost in thought, she waited to speak until they were back at his house. He locked the door behind them and leaned against the wood.

"Flynn, I don't want to put your family and you in danger. I called Trent and left a message. When he calls back, I'll make plans to get back to the mainland."

Flynn shook his head. As if letting her out of his sight was an option. It wasn't. "Mia. I told your brother I'd watch out for you." He pushed off the door and headed in her direction. "I never welch on a bet."

"That bet was made before all this crap started happening. Neither he nor I are holding you to it. This is more than just showing me around the Island and helping me find a house. This guy is dangerous."

"So I gathered." Flynn walked into the kitchen and grabbed two beers from the fridge in one hand, grabbed her hand with his other hand, and led her out the back door down to the lake.

He sat down on the embankment and waited for her to sit with him before he popped the top, handed her that beer, and then opened his own. They sat in silence and watched the sun dance on the water.

"Do you know why I swim in the lake every morning?"

"To stay fit?" she asked as she lifted the bottle to her lips.

"That's just a bonus." He glanced at her. "Some people meditate to calm their mind. I swim. It helps me forget."

"Forget what?"

Flynn took another long swig of his beer. "It doesn't matter," he said as he swiped the dribbles from his chin. "That's not the point. Swimming is my outlet. It's my own personal sanctuary, where no one can touch me. It's just the water and me." He glanced at her. "What's your place? Where do you go?"

She took another swig of her beer. "I work."

He nodded a couple times, stood, and held out his hand.

"Where are we going?"

"The lab. So you can blow off some steam and find your zone."

She glanced back out at the crystal blue water.

"I'm not your enemy, Mia. Quit fighting me and just trust me. You need to relax."

Her gaze searched his before her whole demeanor softened as she stared up at him. "You aren't going to make me swim?"

He smiled. "Not unless you want to."

She took his hand and let him pull her up. "I think that's exactly what I need to do."

She set her beer down, reached for the hem of her shirt, and lifted it over her head. Her shoes and socks were next. When she reached for the button of her shorts, Flynn sputtered around his beer bottle, choking on the amber liquid.

She slowly lowered them and kicked them to the side, standing in nothing more than black panties and a lace bra.

"What?" she asked as she smiled. "You've seen women in less than this." Mia stepped into the water, leaving him on the shore.

"They weren't you," he whispered to himself and undressed, leaving only his boxers on before he joined her.

She ducked under water, soaking her head. Coming up, she wiped the water from her face and looked up to the sun. She closed her eyes.

"I came here to experience the Island, and this is living."

Flynn walked in up to his thighs and dived in the rest of the way, resurfacing where she was treading water. "You're just full of surprises, Doc."

He stood in front of her, and she wrapped her arms around his neck and her legs around his waist.

"My time here is limited." She visibly swallowed. "I don't want to die tomorrow and have any regrets."

Flynn rested his palms on her waist and tried to tamp down his libido. "You aren't going to die tomorrow, but I'm all for you having no regrets."

Her gaze washed over his face and landed on his lips, and he knew what she was thinking. What she wanted. She was on the verge of giving in to their chemistry.

"You don't know that," she whispered a second before she pressed her soft lips to his.

He took what she so freely gave and deepened the kiss. Stroking his tongue against hers. Tasting and savoring the moment, unsure when it might happen again. She strained against him, pulling him closer, and it took all of his resolve to not just take her, here in the water where it was just the two of them.

His cock hardened in response as she ground against him.

"Mia." He broke the kiss and held her gaze. "Why now?"

Her brows dipped at his question.

"Not that I don't want to or that we won't. I just need to know where your head is. If you're doing this because you're scared, you don't need to be."

She stiffened in his arms.

"You need to feel in control, don't you? Your life is spiraling out of control, and this is one place where you have the say."

"You don't know what you're talking about." She pushed against him, and he let her go to disappear beneath the water.

He followed behind her, and when she resurfaced, he was standing behind her in waist-deep water. He turned her to face him. "I'm not trying to upset you."

"Really?" She lifted a brow. "Flynn, quit playing games with me. If you don't want me, just say so."

"Games?" He pulled her closer, bringing their bodies flush against each other so she could feel exactly what she was doing to him. "Does this feel like I'm not attracted to you?"

Her breath quickened and her chest heaved. Her cheeks flushed, either from the sun or his proximity. He didn't know which. He knew exactly why his body was burning.

"Don't patronize me." Her voice lacked conviction and the fire she'd shown him over the last few days.

"I wouldn't dream of it," he said before he kissed her back, tasting and taking again, only this time, on his terms. He gently slowed the kiss and broke the connection, cupping her cheek. "When I take you," — he smiled — "and I will take you, it won't be because you're scared and ready to run again. It will be because you want me as much as I want you." He kissed her neck. "And not a moment before that."

He kept her in his arms and walked her farther into the water. He ran his fingers through her wet hair, his hold on her hip strong and firm. He knew what she needed, even if he wanted more. He couldn't give her what she asked, but he could give her this.

He lifted her and walked deeper into the water. Her legs wound around his waist as his palms cupped her butt. He kneaded her ass cheeks while slipping his fingers beneath the elastic of her panties.

She moaned, and her body relaxed in his hold before he took her lips again, this time in a slow exploration as he held her with one hand. His other fingers moved farther beneath her panties, touching her flesh in the most intimate places.

He slid his fingers over her folds, and she broke the kiss and moved against the motion.

Flynn grinned. "Don't worry. I'll give you what you need." He kissed her neck. "Always what you need, even if it's not what you want," he whispered as he kissed his way up her neck.

He slid a finger inside her, stroking her heated channel. She moved her hips against his hand, and he added another finger inside her tight sheath. He continued his ministration as she let her head fall back on her shoulders. He held her close and quickened his pace, fighting his own need to be inside her.

She tightened around his fingers, and he knew she was close. Flynn used his teeth to move her bra and ran his tongue around her breast before he took her nipple into his mouth.

She tightened more, and he could feel the little spasms starting. "That's it, baby. Give it to me."

He used his teeth, scraping her creamy globe.

"Yes."

He continued, moving harder, sure he would leave a mark as he quickened his fingers. He circled her clit with his thumb and pressed.

Try as she might to hold in her release, she didn't win. She moaned his name as he worked her over the edge and watched her fall apart in his arms. Watching her gave him a new meaning for the word beautiful. He worked her through the spasms, not stopping until she lifted her head and met his gaze. Her breathing was harsh as she tried to gain control and she bit her lip. Her mind was already back at work, trying to make sense out of what just happened.

"Flynn...."

He shook his head. "Mia." He slid his fingers free and held her by the globes of her ass, not letting her go. "I promise I won't let anything happen to you. Not because of my bet, not because of any other reason except that I need you to be safe."

She held his gaze, and he knew she could see the truth of his words and what he hadn't said. She nodded, and that was all he needed. All he asked for in that moment was that she trust him.

She kissed him, this time not out of fear or thinking she might never get the chance again. She kissed him because she wanted to. He could tell the difference, even if she couldn't, and he couldn't ask for more.

"How about we get you dried off?" Flynn kissed her lips once more. "Then you can tell me everything that happened so we can figure this out."

"What about you?" She tried to wiggle closer, but he held her at bay.

"This was never about me," he answered

and walked toward the shore. When he got waist deep, she slid down his body. He immediately missed her warmth as they walked out and grabbed their beers and clothes.

7 CHAPTER

They walked into the kitchen and froze. Flynn's brother, Declan, and Stan stood in the living room. Stan's gaze dipped down Mia's body, and Declan's brows rose.

Mia moved her clothes to cover herself, to shield their view. Flynn moved her behind him. "Do you mind?"

Stan's jaw ticked. Anger rolled off him in waves, but Declan met Flynn's gaze with more curiosity than anything else. Declan patted Stan on the back. "We'll be on the porch when you're dressed."

They left, and Mia ran to her room while Flynn tossed on some dry clothes before walking back to the front door, where he pulled it open and left them to follow. He walked into the kitchen and turned on the coffee pot.

"Is that what you call protecting her?" Stan growled.

Flynn glanced over his shoulder, giving Stan the same smirk Flynn had received in the park.

Stan lunged for Flynn, but Declan stopped him. Flynn slowly turned, leaning against the counter as if the detective wasn't even a threat. "She needed to de-stress, and we went swimming."

"Yeah, I just bet that was your idea."

"Actually, it was mine," Mia announced as she bounced off the last stair and turned the corner, moving to stand next to Flynn while waiting for the coffee pot to finish. "What are you doing here, Stan?"

Declan cleared his throat. "Stan got me up to speed on what you've been dealing with, and while we were talking, he got a call about your case."

"Oh?" Her brow rose questionably, and she laced her fingers together, trying to hide the fear.

"The app you use on your phone that tells you distance and location when you jog, you left it on, so they were able to piece together a trace of your phone's route every time it was turned on."

"If her phone was on, then what took you so long tracking it down?" Flynn asked.

"It wasn't on the entire time, but her jogging app helped us locate where the phone went."

"And where did it go?" she asked as Flynn handed her a cup of coffee before he made his own.

"All over town and it was used for several calls, some to known drug dealers, but we expected that when we thought some punk mugged you. That's not what has me worried."

Mia glanced between Stan and Declan. "What has you worried?"

"Mia, at one point, the location popped up at Fuller."

Mia's mouth parted, but she didn't speak.

"What is Fuller?" Flynn asked.

"A psychiatric hospital." Mia's answer came out as a whisper.

"Where Garth Miller was institutionalized," Stan added. He stepped closer to Mia and pulled out one of the kitchenette chairs for her to sit. He took the seat opposite of her. "Mia...he's been released."

"Who is Garth Miller?"

Mia covered her mouth as she took several deep breaths. Terror shined in her eyes.

"Garth Miller is the punk that kidnapped her when she was fifteen."

"Why didn't they throw his ass in jail? Why the institution instead?"

"Extenuating circumstances. He's her biological brother," Stan answered.

"I thought Trent was your brother."

"I was adopted. My parents were the worst kind of people. They were drug users, and they tried to sell me to an undercover cop for drug money."

"And Garth?"

More tears fell down her face, and she swiped at them. "They apparently did the same thing to him before I was born. I didn't even know about him, and unlike me, he was adopted into another abusive family. When he found me, my parents bribed him to leave. They didn't tell me." She closed her eyes and lowered her head as she continued. "I only found out later, when he showed up again after they'd died. He was on drugs when he came to me. He wanted more money, and when I told him I didn't have any, he tried to kidnap me, knowing Trent would figure out a way to pay my ransom. Only he didn't get that far. I escaped."

"Oh, Mia, I'm so sorry."

"We have a call into his case worker, and I have another officer going by his listed address to see if he's where he's supposed to be. A condition of his release was that he not have any contact with you. If he does, he'll go to jail this time."

"The guy at the pool," she whispered to herself and cupped her hands around the coffee mug.

"Mia, what guy?" Flynn asked while sitting next to her as Declan took the seat next to Stan.

"That day of the corporate event when they played volleyball at the hotel, I was up in my room when you were talking to Declan and everyone else. There was a guy across the pool. He was watching me, but it couldn't have been him. He was wearing a suit without a jacket and had sunglasses on. Garth wouldn't dress like that, but this guy stuck out like a sore thumb."

"Why didn't you say something?" Declan asked.

She shrugged. "I thought I was being paranoid." She met his gaze. "I never saw him again after seeing him at the pool. I looked for him, and then later that night, I packed and came here."

Declan slid out of his seat. "We have cameras covering the entire area after what happened with McGregor's daughter." He dialed a number, put the phone to his ear, and paced the kitchen. "I need all the footage for the last three days from the hotel."

Flynn rubbed her back and ignored the hard, cold glares coming from the other side of the table. Masking his annoyance with the detective, he focused his attention on Mia. "Declan will find this guy."

Declan shoved the phone back in his pocket. "I called Reed on the way over here. He'll be here soon to revamp your security system and put up more cameras."

"That's a good idea." Flynn stood.

"Mia, you should come back with me," Stan suggested. "I'm sure your brother would agree."

"She's not going with you. Can't you get that through your thick head?" Flynn blurted out.

"Who asked you?" Stan's lips thinned in irritation, his tone hoarse with frustration.

"I'm not leaving." Mia ignored their exchange. She shook her head and stood, lifting her chin. "I'm done running."

Declan patted Stan's back. "She's in good hands."

"Yeah, we saw how cozy you two were in the lake." Stan glanced at Declan. "He's going to be too busy fucking her to protect her."

Flynn shot out of his seat and lunged around the table. Yanking Stan up from his chair, he shoved him up against the wall.

"Flynn," Declan growled. "Let him go. You hit him, and he'll press charges. Mia doesn't need that right now. She's the one who's important."

"Flynn, don't. He's just worried..." Mia touched his arm.

"Let me be clear, Stan." Flynn's eyes narrowed, his anger no longer in check. This asshole needed to learn a lesson, and Flynn was just man enough to give it to him. "If she still wanted you, she'd be with you. I'm not keeping her prisoner, and she's welcome in my home for as long as she wants. Now you, on the other hand, can get the fuck out of my house."

Flynn pushed off of Stan and stepped back, clenching and unclenching his fists. Flynn's nostrils flared. He was done playing with this schmuck. He didn't care if the dipshit carried a badge. No one talked to him that way. No one.

"You're nothing more than a playboy. She'll get tired of you soon enough."

"You don't know me," Flynn spat back. "You don't know a damn thing about me."

"That's where you're wrong, you little punk." Stan yanked at the hem of his shirt, straightening the fabric. "We've been through her life with a fine tooth comb, including everyone on the Island that she's been in contact with. Trent gave me your name. I've checked your background."

"That's enough." Declan pulled Stan out of Flynn's reach, and with his hand on Stan's chest, he pushed him backward toward the door.

"Did you tell her about your dead girlfriend?"

"Get the fuck out."

Declan shoved Stan out the door and slammed it behind them.

Mia touched his arm, and Flynn shrugged her off. "Mia...I can't right now."

He looked into her eyes and could see the pity and the questions she was holding back. "I just can't."

He left her standing there, stormed off in his room and plopped down on his bed, holding his head between his hands. The memories flooded his mind as though the accident had happened yesterday. He squeezed his head, hoping the memories would vanish again, yet they didn't. He closed his eyes, and a picture of her bloody face and the way her body lay limp and cold flashed into his mind. He took several deep breaths to calm his thoughts. He lifted his gaze, concentrating on the blue water outside. The same vibrant blue that had matched her eyes.

"Flynn." Mia knocked before she opened the door.

"Mia, please..."

He didn't bother to look behind him. He knew what he'd see. The bed depressed next to him, her hand landed on his leg, and she gave a reassuring squeeze.

"You don't have to talk." Her words were quiet in the room. "Just let me be here."

He laid his hand over hers, and they sat like that, for how long he wasn't sure. At some point, she rested her head on his arm and they'd threaded their fingers together. It was a comfortable quiet in a crazy day.

Flynn finally spoke. "He was right. When I was sixteen, my girlfriend died because of me."

Mia remained silent, yet she didn't pull away.

"I..." He swallowed hard around the lump in his throat and ignored the acid churning in his stomach. He let out a deep breath. "Mia." He turned to face her and held her hand. "There's something you should know about me."

She gave him a reassuring nod while squeezing his fingers.

"I have premonitions. I get glimpses of things before they happen. I don't expect you to believe me, but I do, and when I was eighteen, I had one about that accident. I knew it was going to happen. I didn't know why she was going to speed off, but I knew she was going to get into an accident. She showed up at my house and we had a major fight. She left in tears and not in her right mind. I didn't stop her in time." He took a deep breath. "When I finally went after her, I found her car flipped, and she was bleeding from the head. Another driver had run a stop sign and T-boned her car, sending it careening down an embankment." His heart clenched. "Sonja didn't even make it to the hospital, and it was all because of me. I shouldn't have let her run out."

"Flynn, this isn't your fault. You weren't driving that other car."

He shook his head. "I could have taken her keys." He ran his hand over his head. "There are a million things I could have done, but I didn't." Flynn dropped his gaze, unable to look her in the eye any longer. "I'd broken up with her."

"It's not your fault," she said in the quiet room.

"It is. Don't you get it..." He slipped his hand free and stood, walked over to the window, and placed his hands on the glass, staring out at the lake. "I saw it happen."

He laid his forehead against the cool window and closed his eyes. He heard the creak of the bed as she got up. He expected her to leave. He wouldn't blame her if she did.

She wrapped her arms around his waist from behind and laid her head on his back. "You weren't the one who ran the stop sign, and you didn't make her get in that car."

He shook his head, turned in her arms, and pulled her into his embrace, resting his chin on top of her head. "I didn't stop her either."

He'd replayed the day over and over in his mind for years. It was a constant reminder of why he never let anyone get close, never let anyone else back in.

She looked up at him, not with pity in her eyes but understanding. "Shitty things happen to good people. I think we can both attest to that. It's not the heartaches and trials that define us but how we come out of them, and trust me when I tell you, this wasn't your fault. You need to forgive yourself."

Flynn laid his palm on her face. "I had one about you too."

Mia rubbed her lips together but didn't look away.

"You had a gun in a forest of trees, and I took it from you."

"Why would I have a gun? I don't even own a gun."

He shrugged, pulled her back against his chest, and stroked her hair. Something was going to happen. He could feel it in his gut. "The premonition was a warning."

"Well, consider me warned."

He lowered his head and melded his lips with hers. In that one moment, he forgot about their screwed-up day. He pushed all thoughts of Sonja out of his mind and concentrated on this one moment and the woman standing in front of him.

He rested his hands on her hips and pulled her close, pushing the guilt of Sonja's passing back into the box where it belonged. Right now it was just Mia and him. "Mia...we need to plan."

"Later," she mumbled and kissed him again while pulling him over to the bed.

The doorbell rang, interrupting them, and he rested his forehead against hers. "Thanks for earlier, and for trusting me. I can't imagine that was easy for you."

A smile played on her lips when the doorbell rang again. "You can thank my brother and the bet for that."

"I'll have to do that." Flynn took her by the hand and led her into the living room to answer the door.

"Flynn, open up," Reed yelled from the other side. "I'm not going to wait all damn day."

Flynn yanked the door open to find Reed and five other guys on the doorstep.

"About time." He pushed his way in and barked out orders to his entourage, a mix of nerdy guys to handymen wearing tool belts. "I need cameras on the outside and in. I want the command center set up in his office, and I want this shit sealed up tight. No one coming or going without him knowing what's going on."

Reed grabbed one of the guys by the arm. "Inside and out. Got it? I'll handle the tech side. You just get the stuff in place."

They nodded.

"I always knew you were bossy, but this is a new side of you I don't get to see often." Flynn grinned and moved out of the way, tossing his arm around Mia.

"You're more than due for an upgrade in your security, and now's as good a time as any. So you two can relax, stay out of my way and let me do what I do best." Reed met Mia's gaze. "Your ex-boyfriend, the cop, is a real piece of work."

"Finally." Flynn's grin grew bigger. "Someone agrees with me."

"Declan is sending him packing." He patted Flynn on the back. "This is going to take a while, so I've ordered pizzas from Tony's if you want to pick them up."

"Say no more. Let me grab some cash." He glanced at Mia. "You can leave the hat. We're taking the SUV."

8 CHAPTER

Fifteen minutes later, they were out the door and away from the chaos going on inside Flynn's house. Mia kept her gaze out the window on the passing trees and silently wondered if they were the ones from Flynn's premonition. "Are there any other forests on the Island that you would normally be in?"

"I wouldn't normally even be in those. On the off chance I go hiking, it's on the other side of the Island, and the only other trees near where I would be are the ones on my property or at my parents' cabin."

"Do you go there a lot?"

He shook his head. "Not as much as we did when were little, although Skylar and Luke used it as their hideout two years ago when they were trying to figure out who was trying to kill them."

She gave a slow shake of her head. "I remember that. I still can't believe it was Luke's assistant."

"It's always the last person you'd expect." He glanced at her. "Speaking of which. What happened between Stan and you? You know he still has the hots for you."

"We weren't really going anywhere." She glanced at Flynn, and her mind wondered if the same thing would happen with him. "I work *all the time* and he worked weird hours. We just never got to spend time together unless I was in a crises, and that doesn't make for a good relationship. It didn't make sense for us to stay together, so I broke it off."

"And what about me? Do I make sense?"

Mia shook her head and glanced out the passenger window. "You make the least sense." She smiled to herself. "I'm all work and serious; you're all play and good times. We're more like yin and yang."

"You say that like it's a bad thing."

Maybe one day she'd think so, but today wasn't that day. With each new revelation about Flynn, she was figuring him out. Like in her experiments, she was collecting data to make an educated hypothesis, although she wasn't sure yet she had all the pieces to put the puzzle together. She was starting to see what made him the way he was.

"That's my point." She turned her gaze back to him. "I'm the realist and you're the dreamer. I'm not sure we're suited for much more than a causal relationship."

He gave a slow nod. "I'm good at casual." He grinned.

"And I'm not." She'd made a wrong assumption about Flynn when they'd first met. Yes, he was out for a roll in the sack, but she didn't realize the reasoning behind why he acted like that. He was a good guy, only he shielded himself emotionally from people. His game was an act and not an accurate account of the man he was. He was caring; he loved his family, and he'd do anything for a stranger. He wasn't the pompous asshole she'd first thought now that she was finally getting a glimpse of him under her microscope. Flynn had many more layers, deep emotional layers that no other woman had delved beneath. She kept her eyes on the dirt road, afraid if she looked at him he'd know exactly what she was thinking. Her heart clenched, not from his driving, but because of how lonely he must really be. She knew that feeling, and it sucked.

"Flynn, I like you," she blurted out, catching him off guard.

He glanced at her and grinned. "I like you too."

"I've just decided we shouldn't have intercourse."

"Have you now?" He lifted a brow. "Still trying to control everything?"

"I want us to be friends, even after this is over. I think you need me in your life as much as I need you, and sex will ruin it."

Flynn pulled off into a clearing underneath some trees and put the SUV in park, as if he needed a minute to ponder what she'd just said and let the reality sink in.

After a few seconds, he finally turned to her. "I think it's fair to say that you're attracted to me. Am I right?"

"Yes, but..."

He held up his finger, stopping her rebuttal. "Just give me a minute here. Are you not curious to see if I can rock your world?"

"Well, of course, but..."

He tsked and waved his finger, still in the air. "That's all I needed to hear. No pressure."

"Really?"

"Sure. You said we shouldn't have intercourse. That leaves the rest of the playing field wide open." He put the gear in drive, pulled back out onto the road, reached for her hand, and gave a gentle squeeze. "Relax, Mia. I know relaxing might be a foreign concept to you and hard under the circumstances, probably impossible, but you're trying to control the outcome as if you were in a lab."

He glanced at her. "This is real life, honey, and sometimes, if we're lucky, it can get messy, dirty, and orgasmic." He winked. "I promise the latter."

"Flynn."

"I promise not to have *intercourse* with you unless you beg me." He shot her a hundred-watt smile, and the butterflies in her belly danced with delight.

"That should be easy enough." She nodded, sure of herself.

"If you say so."

She spun toward him, nailing him with her gaze. "You took that as a challenge, didn't you?"

He chuckled. "You catch on pretty quick."

"Even after everything I just said?"

"Especially after everything you just said."

Flynn pulled up in front of the pizza place and killed the ignition but didn't move to get out of the car. "Mia."

"Yeah."

He leaned across the seat and placed his lips to hers, taking until he made her moan. "I plan to kiss you again. Are you okay with that?"

She nodded; he righted himself in the seat and reached for the door handle, pausing before he pulled it. He looked at her once again. "I plan to kiss you everywhere," he said in a seductive voice, showing no signs of relenting.

She stirred uneasily in her seat, aroused at just the thought and angry that her body warred with her declaration. She silently stepped out with no reply. What could she say to that? She wasn't naïve. When he kissed her, and she knew he would, she might just let him make good on that promise. Damn him.

Flynn waited for her in front of the SUV, all the playfulness from his face gone as he gazed up and down the street with a serious expression.

He opened the door and led her in with his hand against her lower back, guiding her to the counter. He gave his name and passed over his credit card as his phone rang. He stepped away from her and answered.

"Yeah."

He listened intently for a matter of seconds.

"Yeah, text me the picture. I'll show it to her and call you back."

He hung up and returned to her side. When his phone vibrated again, he enlarged the picture and turned the phone to her. "Was this the guy at the pool?"

She studied it. The guy had on the same shirt, the same sunglass, and the same wrinkled dress pants. A shiver skirted down her spine. "Yeah, that's him."

"Declan is at the hotel and ready to haul him in for questioning. He just wanted to verify that was the guy."

"Do we need to go down there?"

"Not yet." Flynn sent a confirmation text to his brother. "Declan's good at getting to the truth. So it's a waiting game right now."

"Human lie detector."

Flynn grinned. "You're learning." He tossed his arm over her shoulder and waited for the pizza. "You'd be wise to remember that too. The best thing to do with my brother is to deflect his questions. Don't ever answer him dishonestly. He'll know it in a heartbeat, and trust me when I say that he'll pry just to see what you say."

"Sounds like my brother."

"Here you go." Tony placed five pizza boxes on the counter in one pile, and he walked around it, carrying the other five boxes. "I'll help you carry them out if your girl wants to open the back."

"Oh, I'm not his girl."

Tony's eyes lit up and he smiled. "If you say so, sugar."

Flynn handed her the keys and tapped her ass to get her moving before grabbing the other boxes. "She's my girl. She just hasn't realized it yet."

"This one looks pretty smart. I'm sure she'll catch on," Tony agreed.

Mia glanced over her shoulder and narrowed her eyes but didn't disagree. Flynn grinned as he followed her around the SUV where she raised the back window and lowered the tailgate.

****

Five hours later, with the moon high in the evening sky, Mia glanced at all the pizza boxes. The empty ones were stacked by the trashcan, and Flynn was trying to shove others in the fridge. "You're going to be eating pizza for days."

"We," he corrected her. "We're going to be eating pizza for days."

Flynn walked up behind her, moved her hair out of the way, and placed a tiny kiss on her shoulder as he rested his hands on her waist. Against her better judgment, she tilted her head. "Flynn?"

"Hmm?" He kissed up her neck, stopping right below her ear.

"Fighting is futile, isn't it?"

"I promised." He turned her in his arms. "Not until you beg and you're nowhere near the begging point. Now, if you want to give me an hour…I could change that."

"No. I still stand by my decision." She lifted on her tiptoes and kissed him. "I think I'm going to call it a night."

She turned to leave, and he grabbed her arm and swung her back around. "That wasn't a goodnight kiss. This is."

He cupped her cheek and ran his fingers up into her hair. Anticipation had her licking her lips as she stared into his eyes, waiting and wondering what he would do next. He tilted her head as he lowered his lips slowly to hers with sheer finesse. His tongue danced with hers as he eased her back against the counter, pressing his hard body against hers. He inched his leg between hers and made a rubbing motion. She succumbed to his caress, her core heating, her cares forgotten. He swallowed her moans as he held her in place and moved from her lips, kissing a wet path down to the sensitive skin where her neck met her shoulder. Heat pooled in her belly as she held on to his waist, afraid if she let go she might just fall. Pleasure radiated, short-circuiting her senses, she felt nothing but the tingling in her body as he worked her with precision.

He slowed the caress of his knee against her heated core and kissed her once more. "Good night, Mia." He stepped back, his lips tilted in a playful smile. "Sweet dreams."

"That was just wrong."

Flynn clasped his hands together. The angelic look wasn't working for him. He knew he was playing with fire and damned if he didn't know how to light the match. "I could continue, but that would lead me into taking you on the counter, and that would break my promise."

She gave him a saucy smile and headed towards the stairs, pausing on the bottom step. "I can finish myself." She winked and hurried upstairs. She walked into the room and shut the door, leaning against it, trying to find her composure and cool her heated skin, ignoring the crazy thumping of her heart and the burning desire of her body. "He won't win."

9 CHAPTER

Mia woke up after a fitful night's sleep to someone rapping on her door.

"Mia," Flynn called from the other side.

"Yeah." Mia swallowed around her sticky throat. "Come in."

Flynn opened the door while running a towel over his wet head and dripping swim shorts. "Declan is on his way over and wants to talk to you."

Mia lifted to her elbows, and the comforter fell to her waist. The strap of her camisole hung down over one shoulder, giving Flynn a provocative view. His heated gaze lowered, and her heartbeat quickened. She knew exactly what he was thinking, because she was thinking it too.

She sat up the rest of the way and pulled the strap back up and into place. "Sorry."

"Don't be." A smile split his lips as he turned to leave, only pausing to close the door. "Sleepy-eyed and half-dressed is a good look for you. I look forward to being the reason why."

He chuckled as he closed her door. She could hear him whistling as he headed down the hall. She groaned, fell back against her pillow, and laid her hand over her forehead, trying hard to erase the erotic dream he'd starred in. He was slowly easing under her skin and skewing her thoughts. She needed to find a new place to live and soon. Otherwise, she might just be the one begging.

Mia got up and took a quick shower, emerging from her room put together, confident and ready for the day. She put on her brave face, feeling much more pulled together as she met Declan and Flynn in the kitchen, where she found them having easy brotherly banter. Declan was fixing a cup of coffee when Flynn handed her a cup already made. "Thank you."

Declan glanced over his shoulder. "Just the woman I needed to see." He finished doctoring up his coffee before he sat down at the table. "Why don't you have a seat."

She slid into the chair, every nerve fiber strung tight, not knowing what type of new information he might have. "Flynn said you picked up the guy from the pool?"

"We sure did." Declan let out a long breath. "He wasn't your brother, but it turns out you were somewhat right. The guy was watching you."

"I don't understand." Mia cupped her warm mug, letting the warmth seep into her chilled body. "Who is he?"

"He's a headhunter and hired muscle for McGregor."

Mia took a sip of the hot liquid and savored it as it slid down her throat. "It's no secret McGregor wants me on his team. He's approached me before, and I kindly declined. He wants my research. Any reason to suspect that this headhunter is the guy behind my break-ins and mugging?" she asked, curious if maybe they were looking specifically for any research she had. The thought alone made her see red.

"He's not. He has an alibi, and he's telling the truth. He was here to try to convince you that McGregor would be a better option than working for Luke. He was here on the up and up."

"And you're sure?" she asked.

"I personally questioned him," Declan answered, as if that was proof enough. "Stan went back to the mainland to check his alibi, but I already know that it's solid."

"Human lie detector," she mumbled, and Declan shot his brother a glare.

"What? She needed to know."

Declan's brow rose, but he didn't push for a further explanation.

"Any news on my brother? Have you talked to his case worker?"

"Stan told me this morning that he got that call last night. Garth is accounted for."

Relief flooded her body and her shoulders relaxed. "That's a relief." She glanced between them both. "So there's no reason to believe that anyone followed me. I can get back to life as normal."

Declan hesitated with an answer.

"What? What aren't you telling me?"

"Well, it's too early to tell if it's related, but we did find an abandoned boat on the other side of the Island. We're running the registration and dusting for prints. It could be nothing."

"But it could be something?" Flynn asked as he moved behind her and rested his hand on her shoulder.

"It's probably unrelated, but we're still going to run it down."

"Thank you." Mia reached across the table and placed her hand on Declan's. "I can't tell you how relieved I am that Garth isn't here and no one on the Island is out to get me."

She slid her hand free and put it on top of Flynn's which rested on her shoulder. She glanced up at him. "Just think, I'll be out of your hair in no time now that I can get back to finding a place to live."

"Just keep your eyes open and you two stay alert for anyone suspicious." Declan rose and took his cup to the sink. "I'll be in touch when I have any information on the boat, and when I actually lay eyes on Garth's records."

Flynn walked his brother to the door and spun around with a big grin on his face. He rubbed his hands together, and his eyes sparkled with new life. "This calls for a celebration."

"What do you have in mind?" she asked, feeling as though the weight of the world had been lifted off her shoulders.

"Dinner tonight at LaAmour on me."

"Still trying to seduce me?"

"Good food, good wine, and even better company." He shrugged. "What's not to love about that?" He walked over to the sink and rinsed his brother's mug out.

Mia rose with her coffee cup in hand. "I should go text my brother and let him know I'm okay."

"That's a good idea. I've got some work-related errands to run, so why don't you relax for a while? Maybe enjoy the hot tub or take a dip in the lake now that you can breathe a sigh of relief."

"I might just do that." She grinned and spun on her heels, heading back to her room.

"I'll leave my number on the fridge, in case you need something or just miss me," Flynn called out after her.

Mia waved her hand in acknowledgment as she turned the corner to head upstairs. A relaxing day was sounding better by the moment, although she still had a lot to take care of. Finding her own place was at the top of her list.

Mia pulled out her laptop and did a quick search of local properties for rent and found a new listing on Main Street above Tony's Pizzeria where Flynn and she had already visited. It was a two bedroom. Granted, there wouldn't be a view of the beach, but she could make it work while she looked for something more permanent after the tourist season was over. She called the number on the ad and arranged to see it.

Hurrying out of her room, she caught Flynn before he left. "Can I borrow one of your cars? Trent texted me earlier that he's having my car delivered in a day or two, but I need to run an errand later."

"Sure." He smiled as he pulled the front door open. "The keys are hanging up next to the fridge. I'm taking the Jeep, so you're more than welcome to use the SUV unless you'd rather ride the motorcycle."

"You have a motorcycle too?" She shook her head. "Never mind, of course, you do." He was single and sexy, and of course, he'd have something to complete his bad-boy image. "Thanks."

Flynn closed the distance between them and pressed his lips to hers in a kiss that left her hot and bothered. It firmed her resolve on why she needed to leave.

"Be careful while you're out."

"I'm always careful."

10 CHAPTER

Mia pulled up outside of Tony's pizza shop and killed the ignition. She was doing this. She took a moment and grabbed her purse. Once she committed to a place, she'd be here for at least an entire year before purchasing a more permanent place. Just long enough to, hopefully, finish her research and give the creep that mugged her time to forget her face.

She stepped out of the car, and the hairs on the back of her neck stood on end. She could feel eyes on her. She slowly turned in place, trying to locate the source of unease. Families walked up and down the street, and patrons came and went from the pizza place. She might not know the locals like Flynn, but she thought herself smart enough to notice someone out of place. Nothing caught her attention, but she hurried inside the restaurant anyway, feeling more secure behind closed doors. The aroma of freshly made pizza teased her nose, and her stomach grumbled in delight. Customers were scattered around at different tables, and a guy was behind the counter tossing the pizza dough up into the air. A smile split her lips as she headed for the cash register and asked for Tony.

Tony walked with her outside and showed her around the brick building to the stairs at the back of the shop. "You can park here and come up the back way or you can go in through the restaurant. There are two separate entrances. The choice is yours." He pointed to the lighted area, and it eased some of her concerns.

"Who used to live here?" she asked.

"My niece, Avery, used it on the rare chance she was in town," he was quick to answer. "She's a firecracker, always on the go, and a bit of a fitness buff. It was only temporary while she bought a place down on the beach. She's gone a lot of the time traveling."

"Her loss is my gain."

Tony showed her around the two-bedroom apartment. It was more upscale than she thought she'd be walking into. It had hardwood floors and granite countertops. It was more than big enough for Trent and her whenever he decided to come for a visit, and even better was the fact that it had a security system already installed.

"I'll be looking for a more permanent place after tourist season. I hope it's okay that this won't be long term."

"Not a problem." He walked her back outside and pointed to a row of townhouses across the street. "My nephews live over there, and they like to keep an eye on the place. I'll have to introduce you."

"That's so sweet."

"We're a protective bunch, so you shouldn't have any problems here, but if you do, all you have to do is holler. There are always a couple of us close by."

"That sounds perfect." She nibbled on her bottom lip while she opened one of the cabinets, checking out the exquisite workmanship. "This place is great. The work is so detailed." She closed the cabinet. "Who made these? If you don't mind my asking."

"Jackson Love. He's the best in the business and a good kid, not to mention that he's single if you decide that Flynn's too rowdy for you."

"Is that another one of Flynn's brothers I haven't met?"

"His cousin. There are five more Loves on the Island besides Flynn's immediate family. His ancestors founded the Island."

Mia's cheeks heated at the suggestion of hooking up with another Love relative. The one Love she was living with was plenty for her. "I'm here to work, so you won't find me having any parties or many people over. Maybe an occasional visit from my brother."

Tony showed her the other exit down into the restaurant, where she was quick to sign on the dotted line and give him a check. He had cleaners coming in a week and told her she could move in next Sunday. With keys in her hand and a skip in her step, she thanked him and left.

Getting into the SUV, she shot a text off to her brother, letting him know that she'd found the perfect temporary place and it was fully furnished, so she'd be keeping most of her things in storage until she found a house. Mia headed back to Flynn's and bit her lip the entire way. She was excited about moving out, but leaving Flynn left an odd sensation in the pit of her stomach. She tried rationalizing the feeling in her mind. The move was inevitable. He'd be happy to have her out of his hair and still living close enough that he could hold up his end of the bet. "You're being ridiculous," she scolded herself. "You aren't even dating the guy."

She tried convincing herself that he'd be better off. He could get back to his old ways, back to the bars and the bimbos, and she could get back to work.

She parked the SUV and killed the ignition as she glanced up at Flynn's beautiful, but empty house, and for the first time since arriving, she felt alone.

Flynn's house was quiet as she entered and turned off the alarm, relocking the door behind her. She shot off a text to Luke letting him know that she was stopping by the office on Sunday to get things in order and she was ready to get back to work. With no reason to fear she'd been followed, it was time to get back to her work. She was on the verge of finding the cure.

Mia changed into her bathing suit and grabbed a towel from the linen closet before stepping out onto the back porch. She ran her hand through the water in the hot tub before turning it on. A nice, long, relaxing soak was well overdue and much needed.

****

Flynn stepped out onto the porch in his swim trunks with a playful grin on his lips. She could read his every intention in his lust-filled eyes. He set his beer on the side and climbed in, gliding through the water. His leg brushed against her silky-smooth thigh. Without a word, he brushed his lips against her bare shoulder, leaving her breathless and lost for words.

"Did you miss me?" he asked in a soft, seductive tone.

His fingers slid across the swell of her breast, leaving her deliciously warm and wet as he eased back, claiming his seat.

Mia swallowed around her apprehension and licked her lips. Her voice came out a mere whisper. "Was I supposed to?"

Laughter danced in his baby blue eyes, and a smile split his lips. "I guess not." Flynn laid his head back against the edge. "Did you get all your errands run?" He turned to look at her.

"I did." She left out the details of her afternoon. "Thanks for letting me use your car."

"So I was thinking..." His fingers left her body, and he scooted to the other side of the tub to face her. "How about we do a nice dinner in, just the two of us?"

Water dripped down his chest, and her resolve crumbled at that moment. She couldn't think of anything better than just the two of them, all alone in this big beautiful house.

"Come here," Flynn said with a concerned tone and held out his hand.

She slipped her fingers into his.

He pulled her across the tub, and she straddled his lap, unable to look him in the eyes. Was she really going to do this? She lifted her gaze as her heart raced.

"What's wrong? Was it something I said? Because you know I tend to put my foot in my mouth."

Heat pooled in her belly as she felt the bulge between his thighs. His hands rested securely on her hips.

"You were right, okay?" she barked out angry with herself.

"That's a first." His eyes sparked as the heat surrounded them. "What was I right about?"

"You're going to make me say it?"

"Baby, you're talking in riddles."

"I want you, okay?"

"You do?" His brows dipped as he held her gaze. "Are you sure?"

Mia reached around her neck, slipped the strings free, and let them drop into the water. "Yeah, I'm sure."

Flynn kissed the pulse on her neck and worked his way up to her ear as he pulled her body flush with his. He whispered, "What changed?"

Her body trembled in his arms, not from fright, but from the way he held her so close, the way he could read her like an open book. His touch promised things to come, yet he was smart enough to question the timing.

Instead of answering, she reached between them and stroked his erection through the fabric of his shorts. He placed his hand over hers and moved it out of the way, settling her body to where she was straddling his erection between her thighs. "You haven't answered my question."

Her brows dipped, and she reached for the strings of her top and retied them. "If you don't want me…"

"Oh, I want you." He kissed her, cutting off her response until her body relaxed in his arms. He rose, holding her until she slid down his body. "Come with me."

He got out and held out his hand for her to climb over the edge. When she did, he slid his towel slowly down her body, taking his time to dry off her most sensitive parts. When he finished drying her, he dried himself.

Taking her by the hand, he led her back into the house and down the hall to his room. He closed the door behind them and leaned against the wood, blocking her exit. "I promised not to have sex with you, and in the course of me being gone for three hours, you're all of a sudden ready? Start talking."

****

Mia folded her arms across her chest and met his gaze. She was heated again, not from his caresses but from his questioning. "You know what? This isn't going to work." She tossed her arms up; her heart thumped erratically.

"Just answer my question, Mia."

"I found an apartment."

"What? And you thought you'd never see me again? Is that what this is? It was either now or never?"

"No....Yes...shit." She turned her back to him to look out the window. "No." She finally turned back. "I don't know what will happen after I leave." Her shoulders sagged. "I like you. I really like you."

"Now, was that so hard? I like you too." Within seconds, he had her on the bed, his large body splayed between her thighs. The silky sheets caressed her barely covered skin. He kissed her thoroughly and deeply, and her body heated, every one of her nerves aware and waiting for what she hoped was next.

"I promised to make you beg," he whispered against her lips. His blue eyes turned a storm gray as he left her mouth and kissed a path down her chest. Moving the cup of her bathing suit with his fingers, he took her breast in his mouth.

She arched her back in response and held his head to her body, afraid if she let him go that he'd stop. He slid his fingers beneath the material covering the other breast and caressed it while running his tongue over her skin. He sucked her nipple until it stood erect before moving to the other one. Reaching beneath her, he slipped the tie free, pushing the fabric out of the way. She moaned again lifting her thighs, searching for the one thing she'd been longing for.

"Patience," he whispered before he took that nipple in his mouth. Using his tongue and his teeth, within seconds, he had her worked up, ready and wet between her thighs.

"Flynn," she whispered as he kissed a path down her stomach and kissed her core through her suit.

"I promised to make you beg." He glanced up at her with a predatory smile. "And I never go back on my promises."

He slid his fingers between the straps of her bottom and her skin before easing them over her hips and down her legs. He ran his palms up her thighs, opening her up to his gaze as he lowered his head. He blew on her heated skin before running his tongue through her folds.

"Oh God," she whispered and grabbed the sheet, using it as an anchor to keep her grounded.

Parting her folds, he devoured her with his tongue. The exquisite feel of his mouth on her had her lifting her hips for better access. Her muscles tightened as every nerve ending responded to his intimate caress. She rested her hand on his head, holding on to his hair as he worked her body. Tension built through her body, deeper and stronger until her toes curled and she could feel the tremors starting deep inside.

"Flynn, I need you in me," she called out to him.

He slowed his stroking and met her gaze, latching onto her clit. He didn't move.

"Please," she begged, and he slid his tongue in circles. "Please, Flynn," she begged louder and tried to lift her hips, and his hold tightened.

He slipped a finger into her wet channel and twisted it until he found her G-spot. He worked his finger in and out as he pressed down on her nub. Her body instantly spasmed, sending her over the edge. She moaned through her release as he continued to ease her down from her high.

He licked her once more and eased his finger out, sucking the digit into his mouth. He climbed up her body, resting his rock-hard cock between her legs while he reached into the bedside table and pulled out a condom. Sitting back on his legs, he tore into it and held her gaze while slowly rolling the sheath down his length. Her heart raced as she reached for him, winding her arms around him as he lowered to mesh his lips to hers in a kiss that had her ready again and melting in his arms.

He positioned himself at her entrance and held her gaze as he slowly slid every inch into her, stretching her channel and filling her. He closed his eyes and groaned her name while burying his head into her shoulder.

Wrapping her legs around his waist, she lifted her hips, deepening their connection. "Flynn, please."

He eased out of her and lifted his head.

"Baby, this is just round one." He pushed into her, making her gasp, and made good on that promise too.

****

Hours later, they lay in a tangle of arms and legs and out of breath. She gazed out the open curtains while lying across his chest. "The lake is beautiful in the moonlight."

"You're beautiful." He kissed her hair and rubbed lazy circles on her back. "So tell me about the apartment."

"It's above Tony's pizza shop."

"Wait, isn't that where Avery lives?" His fingers paused.

"You know her?" Mia closed her eyes, not wanting to think how he might know her.

"We went out once."

Mia placed a kiss on his chest. "Just once?"

"We knew from the first date that we were better friends than anything else."

"Why is that?"

"She's the female version of me."

Mia tapped his stomach. "That's not nice. You just called her a player."

Flynn chuckled, and the vibration shook her. "No, I didn't, but it's nice to know your honest opinion of me. What I meant was, she's outdoorsy, athletic and has way too much attitude for any one man."

"Oh." Mia sighed.

"So when are you leaving? How much time do we have to enjoy each other?"

"I'm moving in a few days. He made arrangements to have it cleaned."

Flynn rolled, pinning her beneath him, and kissed her deeply. When he pulled away, she could see the gleam in his eye and knew what was about to happen again. Flynn was insatiable with crazy stamina. Her belly growled, making her giggle.

"Come on. Let's get some pizza." He slid off the bed. "We've got to keep up your strength."

He pulled out a pair of his boxers and tossed them to her, along with one of his T-shirts before he slipped into a pair of shorts.

She stood in front of the window looking out at the lake; Flynn had wrapped his arms around her waist from behind. He had just kissed her neck when they both spotted a dark figure running toward the trees.

"Did you see that?" she asked.

He quickly let her go and shoved his shoes on his feet. He grabbed a gun from his drawer and handed it to her. "Stay here and lock the doors."

"I don't know how to use one of these."

He took it from her and turned off the safety. "If anyone comes in, just point and pull the trigger." He hurried to the door and stopped to turn back. "Just make sure it isn't me."

Within seconds, he was gone, and she heard the beep alerting her that he'd left the house. Her heart raced when she spotted him running across the lawn, heading toward the trees. "Crap," she whispered as she hurried to her room and slipped on her shoes. He'd left her with the gun when he was the one who needed it more.

Grabbing her mace, she hurried down the stairs, ran out the back door and into the night, following the same path that Flynn had taken. She held on to the gun with her fingers as far away from the trigger as possible. She entered the tree line and slowed, not sure what to expect.

"Flynn," she whispered and glanced around for any sign of where he might have gone. "Flynn," she whispered louder.

The blood rushing through her ears blocked the forest sounds. She was afraid to move, afraid to breathe, but she pushed in deeper, cringing when she heard the creak of a branch breaking beneath her feet.

An arm wrapped around her waist, and a palm covered her mouth. Her body stiffened.

"Shh. It's me," Flynn whispered in her ear, and relief flooded her body. She nodded, and he removed his hand before slipping the gun free from her grasp. "I told you to stay in the house."

"I'm not going to let you get hurt," she whispered, louder than she'd meant to.

Flynn placed his hand on her back and guided her out of the trees, repeatedly looking over his shoulder until they were back in the house with the doors locked. She followed him as he went around to each of the windows and checked the locks and closed the curtains. "Well, at least I know my premonitions are working. What just happened is what I saw."

He let out a shaky breath, put the gun away, pried the mace from her fingers, and set it down. He pulled her into his arms and held her close. "You good?"

She nodded. "Did you see who it was?"

"No. It was probably just some local teenager because that guy was gone before I made it to the tree lines. He was fast, but I'll check the cameras and see if we can ID him."

She stood on her tiptoes and had just pressed her lips to his when her stomach growled again.

"Come on. We'll heat up the pizza and check the cameras. I think we'll both sleep better with some food and once we figure out if it was a teen."

She slipped her fingers through his and followed him to the kitchen.

Three hours later, after they watched the video and came up empty, their bellies and bodies were fully sated. Mia looked ready to drop on her feet and he took her back to his bed. He lay fully awake while he listened to the sound of her even, steady breathing while she slept. He pulled her closer and tried to relax, knowing she was safe and sound in his arms, but his mind replayed the evening. She was leaving, but it wasn't as though he'd never see her again. She'd just be in town. He pressed a small kiss on her forehead. Would she want to see him again, or was this just sex for her? That was a conversation they still needed to have.

11 CHAPTER

Flynn and Mia spent the rest of the week together. They ate their meals together, watched movies, and savored the remaining time as if they were a couple. Neither one of them talked about how things would change when she left, or even if anything would be different. He spent his days laughing with her and enjoying her company and spent his nights with her wrapped in his arms. The clock was ticking toward her departure, and there was no reason for her to stay. With each new day, they grew closer, talking and getting to know each other to the point where things just meshed between them. He woke up to a glorious, sunny, Saturday morning, and for once in his life, he didn't want to leave his bed to go swim, so he stayed in her arms and closed his eyes just relaxing to the sound of her quiet snore.

His premonition hit hard and fast, making his hold of her tighten as he watched in horror. Mia's face popped in his mind, screaming as she was pulled against a man who had her arm.

"Flynn." He heard her voice. "Wake up."

His eyes shot open, and his harsh breathing slowed. He turned to her. "I wasn't sleeping. That was a premonition, and you can't leave."

"What?" she asked, wiping the sleep from her eyes.

"I had another premonition. You were struggling with someone in a parking lot."

"Did you see who?" she asked, more awake now.

"I didn't see his face."

She leaned up on her elbow and rested her hand on his heart. "There isn't a threat. Your brother confirmed it."

Flynn slid out of the bed and started pacing the room. "Mia, you can't go."

"Flynn." She got out of bed to stop his pacing. "I'm going to be fine. I promise."

She wrapped her arms around his waist and laid her head against his chest. "You're taking me to my apartment, and then I'm going to work. I won't even be there an hour and then I'll tell you what." She looked up into his eyes. "You can pick me up, and we'll go to dinner. How does that sound?"

Flynn cupped her cheeks. "Didn't you hear anything I just said? Something is going to happen. I know it in my gut, and I won't let the same thing happen to you that happened with Sonja."

"Home, work, and you. I promise I won't be loitering in any parking lots or talking to strangers. I'll carry my mace, ready to spray anyone that even looks at me funny. I'll be okay."

"Do you promise? Nowhere but home, work, and me."

"I promise." She slid her hand through his. "Now come take a shower with me." She grinned, giving him a saucy wink over her shoulder while pulling him toward the master bath.

****

Flynn did a thorough search of her apartment and insisted she use the restaurant exit when she left. Once agreed, she kissed him goodbye and locked the door. She dragged her suitcases into her room and had just hoisted them onto the bed when the phone vibrated in her pocket. She glanced at the screen, expecting more safety rules from Flynn, and instead, it was her brother.

Your car is being delivered today.

About time, she replied.

You good? You settled into the new apartment yet?

Just arrived. I need to unpack. Talk tonight?

Ok. Be safe.

Always. Love you.

Love you too.

She slid the phone back into her pocket and had unzipped the suitcase when she heard the alarm beep that someone had entered her apartment. She grabbed her pepper spray and was turning the corner when she found a woman in the hallway.

"Whoa there." The intruder lifted her hands, as if to show she was unarmed. "You must be Mia, Flynn's girl," she said as a statement instead of a question.

"Who are you?"

The woman held out her hand. "I'm Avery, Tony's niece."

Mia lowered the pepper spray and shook Avery's hand.

"I thought you were coming later. I was hoping to be in and out so I didn't bother you."

Mia glanced at the key in Avery's hand. "What are you doing here?"

"Left a bag in the closet." She handed Mia the key and slid past her, walking around as if she owned the place. Mia followed her to the room, where Avery pulled a bag out of the closet. She unzipped it and pulled out a gun before putting it back inside.

"Why do you have that?"

"It's part of the job. I could tell you, but I'd have to kill you." She grinned. "Besides, a girl can never be too careful." Avery glanced at the pepper spray. "Is that your primary source of defense?"

Mia nodded, feeling a little intimidated by Flynn's one-time date. Her short, black hair was styled in a pixie cut, showcasing her emerald eyes. She was dressed in a tight, clingy tank top and a pair of cut-off shorts giving Mia a glimpse of her toned and tanned long legs. The woman was a looker all right. No surprise that Flynn had been attracted. She was strength and beauty, nothing like Mia. Mia prided herself on being smart, but she didn't have a knockout body like this chick.

She slid a card out of her pocket and handed it to Mia. "Come see me and I'll give you some free lessons on how to defend yourself." Avery hoisted the strap over her shoulder. "A girl can never be too careful." Avery walked by her. "Especially with lunatics." She glanced back. "Or spring breakers. I swear those college kids come here just to kill brain cells. They can be a rowdy bunch."

Mia lifted the card. "I sure will. Thanks."

"We girls have to stick together, and since you're renting the place, we're practically family." She wiggled her fingers in the air and left as quickly as she had shown up. "Tootles."

Mia put the key on the dresser, went back into the living room, and relocked the door.

"Wow," she whispered to herself and glanced down at Avery's card. Avery was exactly as Tony had described her. She was a whirlwind of energy all balled up, not to mention she could easily be a body double for Trinity from the Matrix. Mia shoved her pepper spray into her pocket, walked back into the bedroom, and began the grueling task of putting her stuff away. It was three o'clock before she called a cab and headed down into the pizzeria, waiting inside for the cab to pull up out front. She waved to Tony as she walked out and hopped in the cab.

"Tanner Pharmaceuticals, please," she told the cabbie as she slid into the car.

The cab rolled down the street as if he was a tourist and time was on his side. He stopped for pedestrians and managed to hit every light between the pizza shop and the lab. The only good thing to come out of the cab ride was that he dropped her off just outside the door, knocking out one less parking lot she needed to worry about.

Mia paid the cabbie and stepped out, hurrying inside to the safety of her office. She fired off a text to Flynn to let him know where she was and that all was well. By the time she left, she'd be in his company and they could both breathe a sigh of relief.

Mia passed the receptionist desk and headed to the elevator, stabbing the button. The lab was her home. It was where she spent most of her time. The atmosphere was laid-back but professional. Everyone did their own thing, unless they were working in teams. Their sole focus at the Island lab was research, and that was where she excelled. She'd just put her purse away when her desk phone rang.

She hit the speaker button. "Mia Stewart."

"Ms. Stewart, your brother is here with your car."

Mia clasped her hands together. "Great. Tell him I'll be right down."

Mia hung up the phone and headed back down on the elevator. She stepped out into an empty lobby. "Where did he go?"

"He's waiting outside."

"Thanks, Tammy."

Mia hurried across the lobby, excited to see her brother and finally have her car back. She stepped outside into the sun and glanced around the parking lot. She'd taken another step out when she felt fingers digging into her arm and saw a gun pointed at her. She came face to face with her brother, only it was the wrong damn one. "What are you doing here?" she asked and tried to wiggle her arm free.

"Saving you," he answered and pulled her around to the side of the building. "We have to go."

Fear clung to Mia like the heated sun. She dug her feet in and pulled against Garth. He wasn't dealing with the same little girl as before. She remembered the pepper spray in her pocket, but it was on the wrong damn side. "I'm not going anywhere. Just tell me what you want."

His hold tightened. "Stop fighting me. I'm not going to hurt you. This isn't like last time. I'm not on drugs."

She peeled at his fingers until he loosened them. "You could have fooled me. Sane men don't kidnap women."

"I'm not kidnapping you, I'm saving you. You're in danger, and we have to leave. Now!" His eyes narrowed as they darted around their surroundings.

"You're the only one I'm in danger from. Let me go," she pleaded.

12 CHAPTER

Declan was going through the file he'd compiled on Mia and found it incomplete.

"Did we get the prints on that boat yet?" Declan hollered from his office.

"We just got a hit." One of the deputies leaned into the room. "Garth Miller."

Declan's jaw ticced, and he flipped to the back of her file where Garth's paperwork was supposed to be and found it still hadn't arrived. Stan had promised to send the information on her estranged brother, Garth, from Fuller Psychiatric Hospital. He got on the computer and found the contact information for Fuller, only to be told they couldn't discuss

Garth and to talk to his case worker in charge. He was given the number.

Declan hung up and called the officer.

"Swanson."

"Hi, this is Sheriff Declan Love from Love Island. I need to ask you about one of your case files, Garth Miller?"

"Yes. Why? Don't tell me he's slipped up. He'd straightened out his life, was doing well."

The hair on Declan's arms rose. There was something wrong here. He leaned forward and rested his elbows on his desk. "Do you know his whereabouts? His name came up in one of my investigations."

"You'd have to talk to Stan Richards. Garth was signed out under Stan's care about a month ago, and to be honest, I don't know what Stan was thinking he could do. Garth may have had a bad childhood, but he's really straightened up his act." Swanson paused. "Unless he's relapsed and Stan hasn't informed me."

"You're telling me that Garth has been with Stan Richards for over a month?"

"Yeah, why? Are they both in trouble? I had heard that Stan was a bit of a hothead, so I wouldn't be surprised."

"I'll call you back." Declan hung up the phone and rose from his desk. Pulling out his phone, he called Flynn only to have the call go to voicemail. He left a message. "Stan and Garth are working together. Call me back."

Declan stepped out of his office, spewing orders to his staff. "I'm going out to Flynn's house. Someone get me a location on Amelia Stewart. Check her apartment above Tony's Pizzeria, check Tanner Pharmaceuticals. When someone gets eyes on her, put her in protective custody.

Declan pointed to another officer. "You're with me."

****

"Mia, I overheard him," Garth said as he stepped closer. "He's going to kill that Love guy and you."

"Who?" she asked when Garth released her arm. She slid her hand into her pocket and wrapped her fingers around her mace can. "Who's going to kill us?"

"Stan."

She froze on the spot. Ice crawled up her spine, settling into her bones. "No." She shook her head in disbelief. "You're lying."

"Yes, he is. He's headed there now. I overheard his plan a week ago and I came to save you. We've got to go. He'll be looking for you next."

"Where's your car? I've got to go help Flynn."

"We need to run." His voice rose in panic.

"No. I'm not leaving Flynn. Where's your car?" she demanded.

"It's not technically my car. I borrowed it."

"You mean you stole it?"

"I rented it from a local on the other side of the Island."

"I don't care whose it is." She grabbed him by the arm, yanking him through the lot until she stopped in front of an old beat-up pickup. She grabbed his keys and hurried inside. Garth followed on the passenger side. She grabbed her phone from her back pocket and dialed Flynn's number, resting the phone between her ear and her shoulder as she shoved the key into the ignition and sped out of the lot.

The phone went to voice mail. "Flynn, Stan is behind this, not Garth. He's on his way to your house."

She hung up and tossed the phone to her brother. "Call 911, ask for Declan Love." She glanced at him as she took the turn, almost going up on two wheels. "If he's not available, tell dispatch you're calling for me and tell them what you told me."

Garth looked at her as if she'd lost her mind.

"Do it now," she yelled; her voice echoed in the cab.

****

Flynn heard the knock on the door just as he stepped inside from his swim. He ran the towel through his wet hair and pulled the door open.

Stan was standing on his porch. Flynn noticed the unfamiliar car in the driveway.

"What do you want?" Flynn asked as his jaw ticced.

"I brought Mia her car," he answered and glanced behind him.

"You can leave the keys here. She'll be by tonight to pick them up."

"I'm going to need to call a cab back to the ferry. Can I use your phone?"

Flynn tried to release the tension in his neck. "Yeah, hold on and I'll get it."

Flynn turned his back, picked up his phone, and noticed two missed calls. As he turned back around, he saw a gun pointed at his face.

"Nice property," Stan said, shoving Flynn inside the house. He closed the door behind him. "Good place to die."

Flynn held up his hands and stepped back, putting two steps between them, getting ready to make a run for it.

Stan cocked the trigger. "I wouldn't do that if I were you."

Flynn froze on the spot.

Stan nodded toward the back door. "Let's go for a walk."

Flynn turned and headed out the back door; his mind raced, trying to figure out how he would get out of this. Athletic as he was, he might be able to take Stan on in a fist fight, but he was no match against a bullet.

"Why are you doing this?" He headed across the lawn toward the trees.

"Isn't it obvious? She was supposed to run to me. Not you."

Flynn clenched his fist. "You were behind the break-ins and the mugging?"

"You aren't as dumb as I pegged you for."

"If they find me dead, they'll trace the bullet back to you," Flynn said as he walked into the tree line. His eyes darted around for a rock, hell, a stick, anything he could use to defend himself.

"No, they won't." He sadistically grinned. "It's covered in Garth's fingerprints, and I plan to leave it behind."

"And Mia's car? They'll trace you through that."

"I stole it when it got onshore. They'll never be able to point the finger at me, not when the evidence goes up in flames."

Flynn gave a slow nod, and his eyes widened as he caught movement out of the corner of his eyes. Mia was standing near a tree with Flynn's gun clutched in her hand and another man standing beside her.

"It's always the one you least expect." Her words caught Stan by surprise, and he shifted so he could see them both. "I trusted you," she spat out.

"Now, Garth, why the hell did you go and tattle?" Stan narrowed his eyes, raised his gun, and pulled the trigger, hitting Garth in the arm before he swung it back around, aiming it at Flynn. "Drop it, Mia, and I'll let you live." He aimed the gun at Flynn's leg and pulled the trigger. Flynn fell to the ground and clutched his leg. His hands were bloody, yet he held Mia's gaze.

Mia's hands shook as Stan moved to stand over Flynn, the gun pointed at his head. "I said drop it, Mia, or the next one is through his brain."

"Shoot the bastard," Flynn yelled.

"Drop the gun, Mia, and we'll leave. I'll leave him alive."

"Don't do it, Mia," Flynn yelled. "He's lying."

"You're right. He is," Declan said, stepping out from behind a tree near Flynn with his gun trained on Stan. "Put down the weapon."

"Why would I do that?" Stan spat and cocked the trigger to shoot again.

In the next second, a shot rang out and Stan fell to the ground, his eyes wide open as he stared up at the tree line.

Flynn collapsed onto the grass when Declan came to his side. Other officers went straight to Garth, who was squirming on the ground.

"Don't move. You're under arrest."

Mia held out her hands and moved in front of Garth. "He wasn't in on it. He tried to warn me."

They glanced at Declan, now applying pressure to Flynn's leg. Declan nodded, knowing Mia was telling the truth. Ten minutes later, Garth and he were headed into separate ambulances. Mia was torn between which one to get in. Declan decided for her.

"I need to get Garth's statement, and I'll be able to tell if he's telling the truth. I'll feel better if you ride with Flynn until we're sure of his involvement."

"I need to say something to him first." She swiped the tears from her face and walked to her brother's ambulance. She stepped up and squeezed his hand. "Thank you. Thank you." More tears fell when Declan held out his hand to help her out.

"Don't worry. We're all going to the same place. We'll see you there."

****

Flynn rested comfortably in the hospital bed with his leg bandaged up.

"Looks like our dinner plans are canceled." Mia sat by his side and squeezed his hand.

"Look on the bright side. Now you can wear a nurse's uniform and take care of me." He wiggled his brows and grinned.

"We so did not need to hear that," Skylar chided him as she walked into the room followed by Olivia, Luke, and Reed.

"You can say that again," Reed replied.

Mia's cheeks flushed, and she leaned over and kissed Flynn's lips. "We'll talk later?"

"You don't need to leave because of them."

"I'm not." She pressed her lips together, and a worried look covered her face. "I need to go check in Garth."

Mia slid off the bed, and Flynn grabbed her hand. "One good deed doesn't erase what he did."

"I know. I don't trust him yet, but he did the right thing this time."

"This time, what about the next?"

She shrugged. "I'm going to take it one day at a time." She squeezed his hand. "I'll be just fine." She kissed him once more. "I'll come back in a bit."

He nodded and watched her leave, and in that minute, he knew one thing for certain. He was falling in love with Mia.

"I know that look," Skylar waited to announce until Mia was out of the room.

"So do I," Olivia chimed in. "Flynn has fallen for the double major. I never thought I'd see the day."

"Hardy har har," Flynn mocked.

Skylar glanced at Olivia and they shared a devious grin. "He needs a plan. This is uncharted territory for him. We need to help him just like he helped both of us."

"Oh no." Flynn held up his hands in surrender. "Flynn Love doesn't need help with women."

"Glad to see the bullet didn't hit your ego," Reed commented on his way to the door. "I'm going to your house to grab the security footage for Declan. I'll check on you later."

"You're leaving an injured man, with these two? Way to throw me under the bus, brother."

"Brotherly love, man, brotherly love." Reed chuckled and headed for the door.

"Chicken shit. Just you wait. When they're done with me, who do you think is next?" Flynn called out as the hospital door shut.

"Quit being a baby," Skylar teased.

"So what do you think we should start with first, a makeover or manners?"

"Neither." Flynn smirked. "She likes me just fine the way I am."

"You two leave Flynn alone," his mother ordered as she walked into the room.

"Thank you, Momma."

"So when are you proposing to that sweet girl?"

Flynn's mouth dropped open, and Olivia and Skylar chuckled.

"Mom, I've known her two weeks." He gestured to Olivia. "Look how long it took Declan and Luke. I think I've got another good year before I even start considering marriage."

"Oh pish posh, I knew your father for less time than that." She patted Flynn's hand. "A mother knows these things. You two will marry, and Mia will give me grandbabies just like these two." She pointed over her shoulder.

"Shit." Flynn shook his head.

"Language," Flynn's mother scolded.

"First I lose a bet to Trent and now Mia."

"She bet you I was pregnant?" Skylar asked as her lips tilted at the corner. "How did she know? We haven't told anyone besides Olivia and Mom. We were going to announce it on Sunday over lunch."

"That one is beautiful and smart, Flynn. Don't screw it up." His mother rose from his bedside and started ushering Olivia and Skylar out of the room. "Come on, girls. Flynn needs his rest."

13 CHAPTER

Flynn wobbled across his living room ignoring the protest from his leg. He couldn't sit still. He took a deep breath and glanced in the hallway mirror, fixing a stray hair that was out of place. Today was the big day. His stomach churned with uncertainty, and he wiped his sweaty hands on his jeans for the millionth time.

The doorbell rang, making his nerves a jumbled mess. "Here goes nothing."

He pulled the door open to greet Trent Stewart on his doorstep.

"What was so damn urgent?" Trent asked.

Flynn stepped back and let Trent into his house. "Nice place," he said as he glanced around before pointing to his leg. "Sorry about the leg. I knew Stan was an ass but had no idea he was psycho."

"Thanks, but that's not why I called you here."

Trent turned to face Flynn again, his brow dipped in confusion. "Why did you call me? I just got off the ferry, and I haven't even seen Mia yet. Is she here?"

"No." Flynn swallowed his apprehension. "You might want to sit."

Trent shook his head. "No, I think I'll stand. What's going on, Flynn? Did you hurt her feelings? You were supposed to be her friend."

Flynn took a steady breath bracing for Trent's reaction. "Nothing like that. I love your sister."

"Everyone does." Trent glanced around, still confused. "What's not to love about her? She's smart, beautiful, and I'd kill anyone who screws with her. You know that, right?"

Flynn shook his head. "No, you don't understand. I love *love* Mia, as in I'm in love with your sister, as in I'm going to ask her to marry me."

Trent's mouth parted, and the blood drained from his face. "Dude. You weren't supposed to fall in love *love* with her. Your job was to keep the assholes away from her, make sure she met a nice guy."

Flynn held out his arms. "She did."

"You've known her for three weeks. That's not even an entire month." Trent ran his hand through his hair. "Give it time. It'll pass. You'll move on, and so will she."

Flynn shrugged, and a smile split his lips. "When you know, you know, and I know I love Mia, and I think she may love me too."

Trent squeezed his neck. "Has she said that? Have you?"

"Well, no, not technically."

"Well, there you go." Trent dropped his hands to his sides. "It was just the adrenaline from her being in danger. I'm sure once it wears off, you'll start to feel like your old self again."

Flynn shook his head. "Nope. She changed me. I've never wanted just one woman before, but I want her." Flynn shoved his hands in his pockets. "I love her."

"How do you know? Have you ever even been in love?"

Flynn clutched his chest. "I knew the day I thought I was going to die. I knew it down to my soul, Trent. I love Mia with every fiber of my being, and before I tell her, I need you to be okay with where this goes. You're her brother, and I'd never do anything to make her unhappy. I'm asking for your blessing."

Trent walked to the window and stared outside. He crossed his arms over his chest. What was minutes seemed like an eternity as Flynn's heart clenched, he was caught in the balance of Trent's answer. Trent turned and nodded. "If she loves you, I mean really loves you as much as you love her, then you have my blessing."

"Thank you." Flynn breathed a sigh of relief. One Stewart down. Now all he had to do was convince Mia, the most brilliant woman he knew, that loving him would be worth the risk.

Flynn grabbed two beers from the fridge and handed one to Trent; they drank while engaging in an easy banter as he showed Trent his home and property.

***

Flynn spent the rest of the week with Mia and Trent, giving them both the tour he never had the chance to give to Mia. Flynn slipped his fingers through hers and he watched a worried look cross her face as she glanced at her brother, unaware that he knew they were together. Flynn lifted her palm to his lips and placed a tender kiss. "I already told him."

"You did?"

"I hope you don't mind."

"No, I don't mind. I'm just surprised you said something."

Sunday afternoon, Flynn spotted Mia and Trent walking up the drive to his mother's house.

"Nervous?" his mom asked, joining him at the window.

"Nervous, anxious, ready to throw up. All of the above," he corrected her.

His mother patted him on the back. "She loves you. Now go get your girl," she said before leaving him to return to the kitchen.

Go get my girl. That was exactly what he intended to do.

Flynn opened the door and invited them both in. "Hey." He shook Trent's hand before kissing Mia's cheek. "I'm glad you guys could come."

"I've had your dad's cooking. I wouldn't have missed it." Trent chuckled and walked through the living room, heading to where the action was.

Mia went to follow him, but Flynn pulled her back. "Lunch can wait. There's something I have to take care of first."

Mia tilted her head. "What's that?"

Flynn pulled his wallet out, removed a five-dollar bill, and held it out. "Turns out you were right about Sky."

Mia's grin lit up her entire face as she slipped the bill out of his fingers. "I'll take that. It was a pleasure doing business with you."

"One day I'm going to learn not to bet you two."

"I knew you were smart." She winked and went to meet the others out back.

Flynn stepped outside and fell into an easy banter with his family, friends, and Mia. The afternoon progressed through good food, laughter and Skylar and Luke's announcement of her pregnancy.

Their typical routine after a meal of watching sports ended up with them all outside lounging around, enjoying the evening breeze. This was life, exactly what he wanted, and he wanted it with Mia.

Flynn took a deep breath to calm his nerves before turning to Mia. "Mia, we need to talk."

The smile on her lips faltered.

"Mia. I love you."

She glanced around. "You're saying that now?"

Everyone around them quieted.

Flynn cleared his throat. "I know we haven't known each other long, and you were kind of railroaded into living with me for a while, but during that time, I fell in love with you." He stepped closer and cupped her flushed cheeks. "You're so smart, and you're beautiful, you're kind and caring, and every time you walk into the room, my heart starts beating again."

"Flynn, what are you doing?" she whispered and tried to pull him off to the side.

He slipped the little box out of his pocket and opened the lid, showing her the two-carat marquise solitaire. "Mia, will you marry me?"

"No, no, no." She shook her head and stepped back, and his heart sank to his stomach. "This isn't logical. You aren't thinking clearly."

"Mia, baby."

An unshed tear rested in her eyes. "I love you, and sometimes you have to throw logic out the window and go with your heart. You... are my heart. Baby, please." He closed the distance between them. "We can have a long engagement if that makes you feel better, but trust me when I tell you, I'm not going to change my mind."

She glanced at Declan. Declan gave her a knowing smile. "He's being honest."

She glanced at her brother.

"Don't look at me. He asked me first, and I left it completely up to you. You're my baby sister. I just want you to be happy, even if it is with Flynn."

The tear fell free. "This is crazy."

"I don't mind being crazy, as long as it's with you." He slid the ring out of the box and shoved the box back in his pocket. "Amelia Stewart, I love you, and nothing is going to change that, not tomorrow, not fifty years from now. I'll love you forever. Will you marry me?"

She bit her lip as she glanced between him and the ring. Flynn swallowed around the lump in his throat. His palms sweated as he waited for what seemed like an eternity.

She nodded, threw her arms around Flynn's neck, and kissed him with all the force of her passion, and he kissed her back.

"I love you," she whispered against his lips. "I love you."

"Just remember who said it first." He grinned and kissed her again before taking her hand and slipping the ring on her finger.

Cheers broke out around them, and his father popped a bottle of champagne. Where he'd gotten it, Flynn wasn't sure. All he was sure about was that he was indeed the luckiest man alive. He kissed her once more and watched the celebration around him. The women quickly whisked her away to inspect the ring while the men walked to his side.

"You did good," his dad announced and patted him on the back.

"I have to admit, I never thought I'd see the day," Declan said

"Neither did I," Flynn answered and let out a long breath he didn't realize he'd been holding.

"Now you just have to get her to the altar." Trent grinned. "Good luck with that."

Reed tossed in his two cents. "Word of advice, brother. Elope."

Flynn's heart was full with so much pride and love. "I don't think so, Reed. If she wants a wedding, I wouldn't deny her anything."

"You're learning." Luke clinked his glass against Flynn's.

EPILOGUE

Flynn cuddled with his wife on the sofa, watching the embers dance in the fireplace. He pulled her close and kissed her forehead as he fiddled with his wedding ring.

"How was work today?"

"Perfect." She settled into his hold. "They approved the drug for human trials. It won't be long now."

"Beautiful and smart. I'm a lucky guy." He kissed her head.

"You know what I was thinking?" she asked, looking up at him with affection in her eyes.

"What's that, baby? Are you ready for kids?"

"What? No." She returned her gaze to the fire. "I was thinking I haven't met Landon, yet. He didn't come to Sky's wedding. He didn't come to Declan's wedding, and he didn't come to ours. Don't you find that odd?"

Flynn sighed around his heavy heart every time he thought of his brother and what he must be going through. "He was working some mission he can't tell us about."

"Are you sure it's a mission? I mean what exactly does he do?"

"He's Special Forces, and he travels the globe, doing what I'm not sure. He calls himself an analyst, but I think that's just for Mom's benefit because he doesn't want her to worry."

"Hmm." She cuddled closer. "He sounds a lot like Avery."

"You met her?" He glanced down at his wife.

"Once at my old apartment. I think I might have to give her a call to see if she can dig into what is really going on. Maybe she's got some contacts or someone she can ask."

Flynn pulled Mia to straddle his lap. "That's you, always the smart one and thinking of others. I never would have thought to ask her."

"Yeah, well, you didn't see the size of her gun." Mia smiled and leaned down to kiss him.

"I love you," Flynn whispered against her lips.

"I love you too," she whispered back. "Now take me to bed."

"Are you tired?" he asked and eased off the couch. Carrying Mia with her legs wrapped around his waist, he headed for the hall.

"Not in the least." Mia wiggled her brows, making Flynn chuckle with delight, and then he walked faster.

The End.

Text KATE to 313131 and get a text message on release dates or go to her website at www.kateallenton.com and sign up for her newsletter!

Other Books by Kate Allenton

Suggested Reading Order

BENNETT SISTERS BOX SET (Books 1-4 in one bundle, 1218 pages)

INTUITION (Book 1)

TOUCH OF FATE (Book 2)

MIND PLAY (Book 3)

THE RECKONING (Book 4)

REDEMPTION (Book 5)

CHANCE ENCOUNTERS (Book 6)

DESTINED HEARTS (Book 7)

PHANTOM PROTECTORS BOX SET (Books 1-4 in one bundle, 964 pages)

RECKLESS ABANDON (Book 1)

BETRAYAL (Book 2)

UNTAMED (Book 3)

GUIDED LOYALTY (Book 4)

CARRINGTON-HILL INVESTIGATIONS

DECEPTION (Book 1)

DEADLY DESIRE (Book 2)

SHIFTER PARADISE BOX SET
NOT MY SHIFTER/ SINFULLY CURSED

KARMA

SOPHIE MASTERSON SERIES/ DIXON
SECURITY
LIFTING THE VEIL (Book 1)
BEYOND THE VEIL (Book 2)
VEILED INTENTIONS (Book 3)
VEILED THREATS (Book 4)

HELL BOUND
MYSTIC TIDES BOX SET

LOVE SERIES
SKYLAR
DECLAN
FLYNN
REED (COMING SOON)
LANDON (COMING SOON)
ALEXIS (COMING SOON)
TANNER (COMING SOON)
GABE (COMING SOON)
JACKSON (COMING SOON)

KATE ALLENTON

ABOUT THE AUTHOR

Kate has lived in Florida for most of her entire life. She enjoys a quiet life with her husband, Michael and two kids.

Kate has pulled all-nighters finishing her favorite books and also writing them. She says she'll sleep when she's dead or when her muse stops singing off key.

She loves creating worlds full of suspense, secrets, hunky men, kick ass heroines, steamy sex and oh yeah the love of a lifetime. Not to mention an occasional ghost and other supernatural talents thrown into the mix.

Sign up for her newsletters by going to her website.

She loves to hear from her readers by email at KateAllenton@hotmail.com, on Twitter@KateAllenton, and on Facebook at facebook.com/kateallenton.1

Visit her website at www.kateallenton.com